Dear Reader,

When I wrote my Harlequin NASCAR novel *A Chance Worth Taking*, which comes out next month, I suspected Michael McIntyre's father had a riveting story to tell. And I was right!

I wanted Royce McIntyre's experience in *Temporary Nanny* to reflect an injury with which our military troops could relate. My goal was to provide hope during times of trauma.

On the surface, Royce's life doesn't resemble that of a soldier. But he triumphs through challenges a wounded soldier might face.

Katy Garner is a single mother struggling to maintain a career and be the best mom possible. Royce is perhaps the last person on earth she'd initially choose to care for her precious ten-year-old son. But soon she realizes there's more to Royce than meets the eye.

I hope you enjoy Royce and Katy's story!

Yours in reading,
*Carrie Weaver*
www.carrieweaver.com

Carrie loves to hear from readers through her Web site or by snail mail at P.O. Box 6045, Chandler, AZ 85246-6045.

# TEMPORARY NANNY
## *Carrie Weaver*

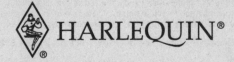

HARLEQUIN®

TORONTO • NEW YORK • LONDON
AMSTERDAM • PARIS • SYDNEY • HAMBURG
STOCKHOLM • ATHENS • TOKYO • MILAN • MADRID
PRAGUE • WARSAW • BUDAPEST • AUCKLAND

ISBN-13: 978-0-373-78192-8
ISBN-10:    0-373-78192-X

TEMPORARY NANNY

This edition published by arrangement with Harlequin Books S.A.

® and TM are trademarks of the publisher. Trademarks indicated with ® are registered in the United States Patent and Trademark Office, the Canadian Trade Marks Office and in other countries.

www.eHarlequin.com

**Printed in U.S.A.**

## ABOUT THE AUTHOR

With two teenage sons, two dogs and three cats, Carrie Weaver often feels she lives in a state called Chaos (not to be confused with Dysfunction Junction, a place she's visited only once or twice). Her books reflect real life and real love, with all the ups, downs and emotion involved, and in 2006 she was a finalist for the Romance Writers of America's prestigious RITA® Award. Please watch for her Harlequin NASCAR novel, *A Chance Worth Taking*, which will be in stores next month.

**Books by Carrie Weaver**

**HARLEQUIN SUPERROMANCE**
1173–THE ROAD TO ECHO POINT
1222–THE SECOND SISTER
1274–THE SECRET WIFE
1311–HOME FOR CHRISTMAS
1346–FOUR LITTLE PROBLEMS
1387–SECRETS IN TEXAS

**HARLEQUIN NASCAR**
NO TIME TO LOSE
A CHANCE WORTH TAKING

Don't miss any of our special offers. Write to us at the following address for information on our newest releases.

Harlequin Reader Service
U.S.: 3010 Walden Ave., P.O. Box 1325, Buffalo, NY 14269
Canadian: P.O. Box 609, Fort Erie, Ont. L2A 5X3

For my mother, Mary Ellen. Love ya lots, Mom!

## Acknowledgment

I'd like to thank Jack Swanson for graciously providing a glimpse into the life of an expatriate in Russia. Any errors are strictly mine.

# *PROLOGUE*

*Russia*

IT WAS A WELDER'S worst nightmare: the odor of gas.

Royce started diving for cover a split second before the force of the explosion knocked him flat.

That's when things began moving in slow motion. Debris rained down on him in waves distorted by the lens of his welding helmet. He grunted as jagged metal tore his flesh. The sound of his coworkers' shouts was muffled by the ringing in his ears.

Dimitri ran to his side and yelled something in Russian.

*Hang on.* Or the Russian equivalent.

Royce tried to respond, but merely groaned.

Dimitri grasped his right hand, telling him

it was going to be okay. But on some level, Royce understood it would never be okay again.

He tried to grasp Dimitri's shoulder, but his fingers wouldn't cooperate. Blinking blood from his eyes, Royce focused. Mangled tissue hung from the wrist where his left hand had once been.

A blessed numbness chased away the pain, but chills racked his body. Then darkness descended.

But not before the irony struck him.

*Damn.*

His ex-wife had been right. He would die chasing an elusive dream.

# CHAPTER ONE

*Phoenix, Arizona*
*Six months later*

ROYCE FUMBLED with his keys. Things came harder these days, even those he was accustomed to doing with one hand.

"You're sure you're up to living alone? You're welcome to stay in the guesthouse." His sister, Becca, pushed her honey-blond bangs out of her eyes. Even nearing forty, she reminded him of an exuberant cheerleader.

"Absolutely not. You've turned your life upside down for me long enough." He silenced her protest with a pointed look.

At last, he maneuvered the key into the lock. He turned the knob, opened the door and gestured expansively with his good hand. His *only* hand. "My palace awaits."

She strode inside and crossed her arms. "This apartment looks exactly like what it is. A furnished place to hide out and feel sorry for yourself. You need a home. You need *my* home."

"Like hell I do. It's about as restful as Grand Central Station. There are kids and pets and old people all over the place."

"Those old people are my in-laws and they're very sweet. My kids can be a pain in the rear, but they'll grow on you."

He couldn't allow her to see how tempting he really found her offer. Wife, mother, businesswoman, caretaker—the last thing she needed was her injured brother taking up space with the rest of her strays.

Touching her arm, he said, "I appreciate the invitation. Really. But I need to do this on my own."

"So why not get an apartment close to me? Or close to Dad in Florida?"

"Dad's started a new life with Evelyn. He spent enough time raising us, he deserves this second chance. Anyway, Phoenix was home before I started the expat life. Maybe I can figure some stuff out here. Besides, you know, the old McIntyre stubbornness."

Becca blew out a breath that ruffled her bangs. Her eyes sparkled with amusement. "I have a passing acquaintance with it. Fortunately, the family curse seems to have passed me by completely."

"Yeah, you keep telling yourself that. I bet Gabe has a whole 'nother story."

"Don't you dare compare notes with my husband. He's hard enough to handle as it is. It's going to make me very uneasy with you clear across the country. Won't you at least let me stay a few days to get you settled?"

"Absolutely not."

Becca sighed. "Then allow Tess to come visit for a while?"

"No way. The last person I need in the middle of my catastrophe is my ex-wife. I have no intention of wrecking her second marriage."

Tilting her head, she asked, "You're not the tiniest bit jealous?"

"No." The truth was, Royce was a bit relieved that Tess had remarried. Knowing she had finally moved on and found happiness put his guilt on a bearable level.

"I don't think I could be as easygoing if Gabe ever remarried."

"Then don't get divorced in the first place." He glanced at his watch. "Speaking of which, I bet your husband is eager for you to get home to start your anniversary festivities. Don't you have a plane to catch?"

Becca touched his cheek with her fingertips. "Royce, I quit being fooled by the tough guy act a long time ago. I know you're hurting, physically and emotionally. I hate leaving you like this, but I guess I understand wanting to do it by yourself. If you need anything, call. Anytime, day or night."

Royce cleared his throat. "You bet. Now get back to your own life."

Becca kissed him on the cheek. "Goodbye, Royce."

Then she turned and walked out the door.

Royce dropped to the couch, fighting emotion.

The silence echoed louder than the explosion.

JAKE TRIED to appear innocent. He looked his mom straight in the eye, though it took all his courage. He didn't want Sally to get in trouble. And he didn't want his mom to worry.

"You be good for Sally today, okay?" She handed him his favorite Diamondbacks baseball cap.

"I'll be very good." There. It wasn't really a lie. He'd just left out the Sally part. She'd called the night before while his mom was in the shower. He'd listened to the voice mail, then deleted it.

"Be sure to ask her to help with your math homework because I might be late."

Jake nodded. A nod wasn't a lie, either.

"Are you sure you don't want me to drive you to school?"

"No. You can drop me off at the bus stop, though."

"You bet." She had that same sad expression when his dad didn't show up to take Jake for the weekend. Like she blamed herself for all the sucky stuff that happened.

He flung his arms around her neck and hugged her hard. Before she could hang on to him and get all mushy, he pushed away and ran to get his backpack. "Let's go."

"Sure, honey. Let's go."

ROYCE CRANKED OPEN an eye and glanced at the clock. The numerals told him it was four o'clock, even if he hadn't already suspected the fact. And the infernal tapping had been going on for at least fifteen minutes.

He should get a broomstick and bang on the ceiling so his upstairs neighbor would get a clue. But he doubted it would work. The noise had started promptly at three forty-five yesterday, too.

Cocking his head, Royce decided it wasn't tap dancing. It sounded almost like Morse code.

*Damn.* If he didn't know better, he'd think his pain medication was making him hallucinate again. But he'd quit taking the meds months ago.

Royce listened intently while he removed a bowl from the kitchen cupboard. Then a spoon from the drawer. He poured cereal and milk.

*Voila!* Dinner.

And who said the one-handed guy couldn't be self-sufficient? Certainly not his physical therapist, Gus, who led him to believe he'd be as good as new with a space-age prosthesis and a crapload of physical and occupational therapy.

The series of taps intruded on his thoughts.

*One-handed man.*

"One-handed man," he murmured, looking heavenward. Was it possible?

"Bring…what? Treats?"

Now he was really losing it. He was imagining an upstairs neighbor tapping out a take-out order in Morse code. And addressing it to the man with one hand.

Last time he'd checked, Royce had been the only one-handed man in the apartment building. Possibly even for miles.

What other explanation could account for the mystery message? There was that cute redhead he'd seen on the elevator. More likely, it was the kid she'd had with her. The boy who looked enough like her to be her son.

More taps.

Definitely bring treats.

Royce booted up his laptop and did an Internet search to refresh his memory of Morse code. When the taps started again, he noted their order, then translated.

"One-handed man. Bring Rice Krispies Treats to 472."

Royce was in apartment 372. But he wasn't interested in playing games with the kid. *Was he?*

Royce thought back to all the afternoons he and Becca had spent home alone while his dad worked. They'd had each other, but it still had gotten old quickly. Wouldn't it have been nice to have someone new break up the monotony?

Absolutely.

Then another thought occurred to him and he was slightly ashamed. But chatting up the kid could lead to meeting his mother.

More tapping. Another request for Rice Krispies Treats.

It kind of tickled Royce's sense of the ridiculous. And the redhead *was* cute.

He grabbed a pencil and paper and figured out the Morse code for what he wanted to say. Then he got the broom from the closet.

Grasping the bristles, he tapped on the ceiling.

*Four-seven-two, you want treats?*

When the tapping started a few moments later, Royce grinned.

"Rice Krispies Treats."

As the tapping continued, he scribbled down the pattern. It translated to, *Homemade.*

He chuckled. "Picky, aren't you?"

But he had to admit, the idea of humoring the kid appealed to him—harmless entertainment to distract both of them.

Royce checked his kitchen cupboards, just to make sure marshmallows hadn't magically appeared. They hadn't. By the time he walked to the corner store and back, he wondered why he'd decided to do this. After the first batch tanked because the bowl kept scooting and he couldn't stir fast enough, he was ready to admit defeat. But dammit, he'd do it no matter what. It was, after all, a simple chore.

And finally, four hours later, he stood outside apartment number 472. He knocked and waited, balancing the covered plate on his left forearm.

He knocked again.

No sound of movement, no strains of a television program. He was too late.

Royce set the paper plate outside the door, trying to ignore his disappointment. It was only a silly game to pass the time.

## CHAPTER TWO

KATY BREATHED a sigh of relief as she unlocked the apartment door. It had been one intense Wednesday.

"Hi, Mom." Jake glanced up from his handheld video game.

"Hi, honey. I missed Sally again?"

"Uh-huh. She left five minutes ago."

"I don't like you being here alone, but I guess five minutes won't hurt." She set her purse and keys on the table next to the door and went to give Jake a kiss on the top of his head. "Still, I should probably call her."

"Sally said it was important for her mom to go for dial—um, to get her blood filtered."

"Well, her mother's dialysis is important. But it's important for you to stay safe, too."

"Aw, nothing's going to happen in five minutes."

"You're probably right. But I want to make sure it's not going to turn into more than that." Between school and her ill mother, Sally had too much on her plate. But Katy's first concern had to be Jake. "I'll call her later."

"She's got class tonight. You don't want to get her in trouble at school."

"I forgot she had class. I'll call her tomorrow from work."

Katy went to the kitchen and retrieved water from the fridge. The chill of the bottle was welcome against her palm. It was only March, but in Phoenix the weather was already warm enough for sundresses.

Jake came into the kitchen, grabbed water of his own and sat on a stool at the breakfast bar.

"How'd the math test go?" she asked.

"I got an A."

"Good job." She gave him a high five. "You're on a roll."

"You want one of these Rice Krispies Treats, Mom?" Jake peeled the plastic wrap from a paper plate she hadn't noticed.

"Did Sally make these?" She bit into one, enjoying the sweet, sticky goodness.

Jake bit into one, too. "Uh-huh," was his muffled reply.

THE REDHEAD barely glanced at Royce when they passed in the parking lot. Though she'd seemed distracted, he'd hoped for some spark of recognition.

Shrugging philosophically, he settled the grocery sack more securely on his hip and headed toward his apartment. Once inside, he went through the now-familiar process of making Rice Krispies Treats.

Royce swore under his breath as the mixing bowl scooted across the counter. He half suspected his upstairs neighbor was on his physical therapist's payroll.

The first batch of snacks had been made only after he'd sat on the floor and braced the bowl between his shoes while he combined the marshmallow mixture with puffed rice.

But there was something almost barbaric about cooking that way. Now, he kept the bowl braced between his stomach and left arm so it wouldn't slide all over the counter.

*Damn.*

His injured arm was still sensitive to pressure. He wiped his face against his shoulder. Who knew a fairly simple task could be such a workout? A year ago, he probably would have laughed at the idea. But now he was seeing things a whole lot differently.

It took at least four times longer than it should have, but finally, he had the treats cut and on a plate. He'd left the first plate two days ago. A coded rave review had come through yesterday. And this morning, a short request for more.

Glancing at his watch, he waited for the afternoon transmission. Three forty-five came and went. No message. What did that mean?

He heard footsteps upstairs.

Royce got out the broomstick and tapped on the ceiling. "U there?"

No answer.

He tapped again and still nothing.

Maybe he'd only heard one set of footsteps instead of two and the boy was home alone. And this wouldn't be the first time he had been left on his own. What if the kid was hurt or something?

A man of action, Royce grabbed the plate of snacks and headed out the door.

KATY GRATED CHEESE for enchiladas with her phone wedged between her chin and shoulder as she talked. "Yes, Mom, I'm concerned, too. I'll talk to Sally about it and make sure she only leaves five minutes before you pick up Jake when I'm out of town. But she's worked for me for three years. I trust her."

A knock sounded at the door.

"I'll get it," Jake hollered.

Katy dropped the cheese, the grater and nearly the phone. She managed to get the speaker covered before she called, "No you don't, Jake."

"Aw, Mom, that's a silly rule."

Katy said, "Mom, I'll have to call you back." She clicked her phone shut and hurried to the door.

"It's probably just someone selling magazines." Jake crossed his arms over his chest, a gesture so reminiscent of Katy's late father she had to smile. "I can tell 'em to get lost as well as you can."

Ruffling his hair, she said, "I bet you can. But it's best if I do."

She opened the door and saw a strange man standing there. A strange, good-looking man holding a plate of Rice Krispies Treats.

"May I help you?"

The man grinned. "These are for you. From 372 to 472."

"Um, thank you."

"I'm the one-handed guy." He held up his left arm and she saw air where there should have been a hand.

"Yes, I…can see that." Katy felt as if she'd been dropped in the middle of a *Twilight Zone* episode.

"I made these especially for you guys. Just like before."

"Before?"

"Ask and you shall receive." He eyed her expectantly as if she should invite him in.

"I think there's some mistake. Maybe you have the wrong apartment."

He glanced at the number on the door.

"Nope. You're 472, I'm 372. Someone's been sending coded messages to me."

Oh, great. Katy bet he wore a tinfoil hat to keep the aliens from interfering with his brain waves, too. Although he looked pretty normal. Other than his injured arm.

"Like I said, I'm sure you're mistaken." Except something about the treats was familiar....

"Just take them. The kid likes them." He extended the plate.

"No, thank you." She started to close the door.

The man planted his size-twelve shoe in the gap.

Recalling a recent burglary nearby, Katy's protective instincts went into overdrive. Especially when she realized this man fit the thief's description.

"Mom—"

She blocked Jake as he moved into view. Making a split-second decision, she brought the heel of her shoe down on the man's instep.

He grunted in pain, cursed and withdrew his foot.

She slammed the door and flicked the

dead bolt. Leaning back, she closed her eyes, relieved when she heard the sound of retreating footsteps.

"Are you okay?"

"Yes, honey, but I should call the police."

"No, don't!" Jake's face was pale, his eyes wide with fear.

"It's all right, the police will find the man and make sure he's not sick or something. And if he's a bad man, they'll take him to jail."

"He's not a bad man! He's my friend."

An awful feeling started in the pit of Katy's stomach. Then she recalled the plate of Rice Krispies Treats they'd had yesterday.

"Jake Garner, is there something you should tell me?"

"He's our neighbor, Mom, so he's not really a stranger and it's okay that I asked him for Rice Krispies Treats."

"You *what?* When?"

"The past couple of days while you've been at work. I got kinda lonely after school. I saw him in the elevator last week and thought it was pretty cool that he only had one hand. I'd been watching Frankenstein and figured maybe he could be somebody's experiment someday and—"

"Get to the point, Jake." How many times had she said that to her son? It seemed like thousands. He had such a vivid imagination.

"I figured maybe he was lonely, too, 'cause nobody looks at him once they notice his hand. They kinda pretend he's not there. And I saw him getting mail one day for apartment 372. He was reading his mail, so he didn't see me."

"So he *is* our downstairs neighbor."

"Yeah. One day I was bored and there were some weird shadows on the wall that made me think of monsters and stuff, so I started tapping out a code on the kitchen floor with a hammer. You know, so somebody would know if the shadows got me."

"Sally would know, wouldn't she? Didn't she object to you pounding on the floor with a hammer?"

"I wasn't pounding, I was tapping."

"Jake," she warned. "What did Sally say?"

"Um, she didn't say anything." Jake looked at the ceiling, the floor and everywhere in between.

She gently grasped his chin. "Out with it."

And the whole story came pouring out. Sally'd had a scheduling conflict this week with her mother's dialysis and Jake had been afraid she might get fired. So he'd decided to soldier on and stay home alone until Katy or her mother got there.

Katy could have smacked her forehead. Why hadn't she seen through his ploy? Because she'd been too preoccupied making a living. And in total denial that her child-care provisions were contingent on everything going as planned.

She grasped Jake's hand and rose. "You are so grounded. But right now, we have an apology to make."

ROYCE SET THE BOTTLE of vodka on the table, along with a glass. His foot throbbed, his left hand itched and his pride screamed for oblivion. Foregoing the glass, he removed the cap and drank straight from the bottle. His throat burned. If he closed his eyes for a moment, the sharp taste of vodka would almost convince him he was back in Russia and none of this had happened. Convince him he was whole again.

But if he kept them closed, he'd start to see the horror and fear on the redhead's face.

A tear trickled down his face. Becca had been right. He didn't have any business living alone and pretending he could lead a normal life. Who'd he been fooling, trying to act as if the explosion hadn't been a big deal? It was the elephant in the corner and the redhead had seen it with searing clarity.

He pushed away the bottle, cradling his head in his hand. No amount of alcohol was going to fix the mess his life had become.

There was a knock at his door, but he ignored it.

Another knock, more insistent this time.

Then a female voice. "Um, Mister, if you're in there I owe you a huge apology. I didn't realize you and my son had struck up a…friendship. Not that I approve of Jake having friendships with adults I don't know, but, well, I just wanted to say I'm sorry. Hope I didn't hurt your foot."

"My mom didn't mean to hurt your feelings, either. She was just surprised is all."

The boy's voice cut cleanly through the door, straight into Royce's soul. The kid seemed to understand that Royce's heart hurt much more than his bruised foot.

Almost against his will, Royce stood and walked over to the door.

Another knock. The boy's voice again. "Mister, we're not gonna leave till we know you're okay."

Slowly, Royce opened the door.

## CHAPTER THREE

KATY CONCENTRATED on the man's deep-
brown eyes, where pain and a hint of anger
lurked. It kept her from staring at his arm.

"I'm Katy Garner and this is my son, Jake.
I'm very sorry for, um, stomping on your
foot and being…rude."

His eyes narrowed, as if he had another
word for her behavior. But he didn't say it.
Instead, he crossed his arms and leaned on
the doorjamb.

"Royce McIntyre. Apology accepted."

Katy hesitated. What now? He'd
accepted her apology. But what about the
pain she'd caused? Could she really erase
it with an apology?"

"Thanks for the Rice Krispies Treats,"
Jake said. "They were really good."

"No problem."

Jake grinned his big, toothy grin. "You're the first adult who's ever gotten my message."

The man shrugged. "Simple Morse code."

"Yeah, but nobody else seems to get it."

Katy interrupted their mutual appreciation. "I guess I overreacted when you shoved your foot in the door. There've been some break-ins in the area lately. I'm still a little uncomfortable with the way you met my son. Jake isn't normally allowed to talk to strangers."

"Hey, he's the one who initiated contact. And how could I know for sure he was a kid?"

"Ask?"

He opened his mouth, then shut it. Shrugging, there was a hint of humor in his eyes. "I guess there's that. I'm not very up on approaching kids, which should come as a great relief to you. Now that you mention it, I see your point about caution." His eyes narrowed. "And yet you allow him to be home alone?"

Katy swallowed hard at the thought of Jake being alone and all the things that could have happened. They'd been fortunate that Royce McIntyre, on second inspection, seemed fairly decent.

Blinking back her frustration, Katy longed for the good old days when situations like this hadn't been a problem. The days when her friend, Karen, had lived across the hall and could pinch-hit during emergencies. But Karen had moved in with her boyfriend across town, leaving a void not easily filled, both as a friend and a backup system.

"We had a communication problem with the sitter and he was alone part of the afternoon this week. I assure you it won't happen again. Thank you for, um, entertaining him."

"Turns out I needed to be entertained, too." He pushed away from the jamb and extended his right hand. "Thanks, Jake. You really had me going."

Jake shook his hand, his eyes as big as silver dollars when they traveled to his left arm. "Were you hurt in the war?"

The man stiffened. "No. A mining accident."

"Jake, that's not a nice thing to ask."

Katy's face warmed. As if the man needed to be reminded of what had to be a traumatic event. From the looks of the tender, pink skin at his wrist, it had been recent trauma. "I'm sorry if he put you on the spot. And I'm sorry I wasn't…more welcoming."

"He has an honest curiosity. Nothing wrong with that. It's better than being ignored…or worse."

*Like being stomped on and having the door slammed in his face.*

There had to be a way to make this better. To somehow undo the hurt she'd caused. Katy shifted, uncomfortable with the solution that came to mind. "Do you like cheese enchiladas?"

He hesitated.

"It's not a trick question. A simple yes or no will do."

His lips twitched. "Yeah, I do."

"Good. I'm making a batch and there's way too much for just two people. I can bring down a…"

The wariness was back in his eyes. As if he thought she was too uncomfortable with his injury to sit across a dinner table from him. How could she tell the man it had nothing to do with him?

"It's okay. I'm good." He started to close the door.

Katy took a deep breath. She had to get past this. If not for her own sake, then for Jake's. She didn't want him to grow up being afraid of every shadow. Cautious yes, afraid no.

She stuck her foot in the gap. "Please come to dinner tonight?"

"It's okay. Really."

"No, it's not okay." She managed a small smile. "Please allow me to do this. We'll eat in, say, forty-five minutes?"

"Goodbye." He nudged her shoe out of the opening with his toe and quietly closed the door.

Was that a yes or a no? She'd assume yes.

"Good. We'll see you in forty-five minutes," she called through the closed door.


ROYCE PAUSED OUTSIDE the Garners' place, a bottle of wine cradled on his left arm.

*What in the hell was he doing here?*

He was tempted to return to his apartment. Nobody had to ever know he'd been here.

But what would he do? Eat another bowl of cold cereal? Then maybe leave another voice mail for Michael? The thought left him feeling so hollow, he knocked on the door before he could change his mind.

The door opened almost instantly.

"Hi, Royce. C'mon in." Jake's hair was plastered damply against his head.

A pang of regret made Royce hesitate. Michael had adopted a similar hairstyle at about the same age. And now his son was a grown man, forging a career in stock-car racing, too busy to return calls from his old man. Or too alienated.

Royce was acutely aware of the passage of time. Funny, but when he'd worked out of the country, he'd sometimes felt as if the rest of the world went on hold until he got back. Children shouldn't grow, parents shouldn't age, ex-wives shouldn't remarry.

Royce suppressed the thought as he followed Jake inside.

Katy hurried into the room, wiping her hands on a kitchen towel.

"Right on time." There was relief in her voice, but her smile was strained.

He handed her the bottle of wine. "I, um, figured it might be okay with enchiladas. But if you don't drink, that's okay, I won't be offended."

"This looks perfect. I'll get wineglasses and you can pour, if that's okay?"

Royce almost broke out into a cold sweat until he remembered the bottle had a twist-off top. By bracing the bottle between his left arm and chest, he could manage. A corkscrew might have required more dexterity than he could currently claim.

Jake watched, his dark eyes solemn. Finally, he asked, "Does it hurt?"

Royce cleared his throat. He wasn't sure how graphic he should be. "Yeah, sometimes. But the weird part is that my left hand itches like crazy. I go to scratch it and realize it's not there anymore."

Jake wrinkled his nose.

Royce glanced at Katy, checking her reaction. No obvious signs of disgust. She seemed to be absorbed in cooking. Her gaze met his, then slid away.

"Did they let you keep it?" the boy asked.

"Keep what?" He turned his attention to

Jake. "My hand? Nope. It was blown to smithereens." So much for not getting too graphic. But the kid had asked.

Jake seemed to digest that information. "Oh."

"Jake, would you please set the table?" Katy handed him three colorful stoneware plates. "Silverware for everyone, then a soda for you. Special occasion."

The kid's whoop of excitement made Royce smile. "It takes so little to make them happy at that age."

"He won't be so excited when I remind him he's grounded for his part in this escapade. He disobeyed the rules."

"I'm sorry I got him in trouble."

"He's usually a good boy, but there are moments when he's a handful. Do you have kids?" She held up a hand. "No, don't answer that. Jake's grilled you enough already."

Royce smiled. "I don't mind. I have a grown son, Michael. We're not close, but I thought I'd reconnect with him while I'm stateside."

"Stateside?"

"Yeah, I was working in Russia when the accident happened. People tend to assume it was something cloak-and-dagger with the Russian Mafia. Truth is, I was welding and there was a propane leak. Sparks from a welder don't mix well with combustibles."

She made a face. "How horrible."

"It wasn't fun. I thought I was dead, so waking up in a German hospital was a real bonus."

"And probably every day after that."

"Not quite…but it's getting better. Jake's been a welcome distraction."

She hesitated. "Why did you answer him? I mean, it's a little unusual for a grown man to play spy with a boy."

"Hey, you don't think I'm some sort of weirdo, do you?"

"No, not at all," she quickly assured him. Almost too quickly.

"In case you have any lingering doubts, I have both Russian and U.S. government clearance for my work abroad. I bet I'm the safest guy on the block, maybe even the state."

"That's good to know." She wiped down the kitchen counter. "Does your son live in Phoenix?"

"Michael's based out of Charlotte. He's busy becoming the next phenomenon of the racing world."

"Wait, you said your name is McIntyre? Is your son *the* Michael McIntyre?"

"Yes. You've heard of him?" Though his voice rang with pride, Royce knew he couldn't take credit for Michael's accomplishments. Tess deserved that.

"Who hasn't? But I'm a Ryan Pearce fan myself. I grew up around cars. My dad was a ringman at car shows and I followed in his footsteps. I help keep track of the bids and bidders and I occasionally do the calling when the auctioneer needs a break."

"I imagine that takes a special talent."

"Talking really, really fast." Laughter transformed her face and made her eyes crinkle at the corners. Combined with her upturned nose, she looked a bit like a mischievous elf. "Seriously, I love what I do, both as ringman and backup auctioneer. It requires a working knowledge of classic cars and the ability to read people, work a crowd, anticipate eventualities. I've heard some people refer to it as a gift."

"I bet."

"The only drawback is the long hours leading up to an auction and the occasional out-of-town event. At first, there weren't many of those. But since we've expanded, I'm spending one, maybe two weekends a month on the road. That makes child-care arrangements tricky. And I hate being away from Jake."

Royce opened his mouth to urge her to make the most of her time with her son, to move heaven and earth to be with him every moment she could. Otherwise, she'd wake up and Jake would be grown and gone. But he didn't usually give unsolicited advice.

"I guess that makes life complex," he said instead.

She nodded. "I have a part-time nanny who coordinates with my mom. I'm lucky I was able to work something out between the two of them. Otherwise it would cost me an arm and a leg."

"No doubt." He'd never really thought about child care. But he bet Tess sure had. More and more, he realized how much he owed her. And thought she had more to show for her life than all his adventures in foreign lands. She'd raised a terrific son, while Royce had let go of everything that mattered.

"Are you okay?" Katy asked.

"Yes, fine." He smiled, trying to chase away his regrets.

Katy got pot holders from a drawer and removed the enchiladas from the oven.

Inhaling, Royce said, "Man, I haven't smelled anything that good in a long time."

Katy grinned. "Flattery will get you everywhere."

He raised an eyebrow.

"In a platonic way."

"Too bad. The other way's a lot more fun." Flirtations had always been a handy distraction in the past.

But Katy didn't seem to think so, he could tell. Her posture was wary.

"Sorry, I was out of line." Royce hurried to reassure her. "I've forgotten what it's like outside the ex-pat world."

Her stance relaxed. "I can always use another friend. Romance is out of the question."

Royce opened his mouth to ask her why, then shut it. It was none of his business. And it was time he faced his problems instead of trying to lose himself in the closest woman who smelled nice.

"Dinner's ready. Would you mind getting the salad out of the fridge, Royce?"

"Sure." He liked that she treated him like anyone else. It made it easier to pretend he *was* like anyone else. Removing a green salad from the refrigerator, he placed it on the table next to the pan of enchiladas. There were already steaming bowls of Mexican-style rice and refried beans out.

"Jake, dinner's ready," she called. Turning to Royce, she said, "We're pretty informal. Serve yourself and have a seat."

Jake walked into the kitchen, then stood, waiting patiently. Either Mexican food wasn't the kid's favorite or Katy had done a good job teaching him manners.

Royce's stomach growled as he loaded his plate. "You don't know how long I've been waiting for this. There isn't much good Mexican food in Russia."

"You've been to Russia? What's it like? Is it freezing all the time? Are there really babushkas?" Jake paused to take a breath.

Katy frowned as they sat at the homey table. "Whoa, Jake, give the man a chance to sit down. One question at a time."

Royce's brain ached from the effort of crafting answers that would satisfy the boy. "Yes, I lived in Russia for several years. It's pretty darn cold all over, but particularly in Siberia. And there are babushkas. In the larger cities, the less fortunate ones beg."

"Beg for what?"

"Money, food, whatever they can get."

"Wow." Jake's eyes were wide as he processed the information. "I want to go there someday."

"The people are warm and practical. They've lived through some rough times, but they keep plugging along."

"I'd miss my mom if I went that far away. Did you miss your mom?"

Royce cleared his throat. "No, my mom died when I was about your age."

"I'm sorry," Katy murmured.

"Who raised you?" Jake asked.

"Jake—"

"It's okay," Royce said. "My dad raised me and my younger sister. I missed my mom a lot at first, but after a while I got used to it."

"I bet your dad played catch with you. Do you like sports?" Jake asked.

"Sure. Basketball, soccer, hockey…"

"Baseball?"

"Of course. Who doesn't?"

"It's fun. But I get picked last for the teams at school."

"That sucks." Royce was trying hard to relate. Most things had come easily to him as a kid, baseball being no different.

"Yeah, it does suck. I'm picked last because I throw like a girl and don't know how to bat."

Katy patted his hand. "I'll play catch with you tomorrow. We can work on that throwing."

Jake wrinkled his nose. "You throw like a girl, too." He turned to Royce. "Will you teach me?"

"Sorry, kid, I don't play catch these days." He raised his left arm. "Kind of hard one-handed."

"It only takes one hand."

"I'm sorry." Royce shifted in his chair. A few Rice Krispies Treats were one thing, regular outings another. There was no way he wanted the kid depending on him like that. "I'm just not the guy for the job."

*Never had been, never would be.*

# CHAPTER FOUR

ROYCE RESOLUTELY IGNORED the tapping on his ceiling. It had been over a week since he'd had dinner with Katy and Jake; he had no intention of becoming Jake's substitute daddy.

Not that Katy had given any indication she would endorse such a plan. On the contrary, he'd gotten the impression she'd been nearly as uncomfortable as he. And whenever they met up in the elevator, conversation had been polite, nothing more.

More tapping.

*R-O-Y-C-E.*

Not gonna bite. The kid was wasting his time.

*R-O-Y-C-E.*

Surely Katy wasn't encouraging Jake? Maybe she didn't know. How could she not know? Unless she wasn't home. What in the heck was the kid doing home at two o'clock on a school day?

There was a thud from upstairs.

Royce stood, grabbing the broom from beside the couch. He refused to think about why he still had it handy.

He tapped out a quick message.

*U O-K?*

Nothing. No footsteps, no thumps or bumps. And certainly no responding code.

He waited a few moments and tried again. When he didn't get a response, he dropped the broom and headed out the door.

Jake opened the door to apartment 472 almost before Royce was done knocking. His smile was wide. "Took you long enough."

"What the hell?"

Jake shrugged. "You wouldn't answer and I'm not supposed to leave the apartment alone."

That's when Royce noticed the baseball glove and ball. "Uh-uh. No way, Jake. I already told you. Besides, aren't you grounded?"

The boy stepped into the hallway and closed the door behind him, using a key dangling from a lanyard to lock it. "Not anymore. Come on, let's go."

"You're not listening. I'm not your baseball buddy. Now that I know you're safe, I'm heading home."

Jake stopped and eyed him. "I guess I'll go by myself then. That'll make my mom mad and I'll probably get grounded again." He sighed heavily. "But a guy's gotta do what a guy's gotta do."

Royce could remember many activities he'd missed because his dad was at work. "Look, I was a kid once, too. I can understand you wanting to get out and play while the weather's great. But—"

"I bet you got to play baseball when you were a kid. And didn't have to stay in the stinking apartment every day."

"Most of the time, as long as I behaved myself. It's different these days."

"No stranger's gonna steal me. I'll kick him hard in the privates if he even tries. You don't have to worry about me. See ya later."

Oh, great, now he'd

Jake being kidnapped by a pedophile hanging over his head.

"Why don't you wait till your mom gets home? She'll be here soon, won't she?"

Jake shrugged. "Yeah. Pretty soon. You know, she won't mind if I'm with you, 'cause you got all that government spy clearance and stuff."

"Not spy clearance. Just a background check."

"See ya."

The boy trudged toward the elevator.

Royce wondered why he was allowing a ten-year-old boy to best him. Sighing, he realized it didn't matter. He couldn't stand the thought of something happening because he didn't want to get involved. What if it had been Michael?

He trotted to catch up with Jake. "Just today. That's it. You left your mom a note, didn't you?"

"Sure."

KATY GLANCED at her watch as she answered her cell. She really didn't need the interruption from her mother now. If she kept her nose to the grindstone, she just might finish work in time to pick up Jake from school.

"Hi, Mom, I'm right in the middle of something, can I call you back?"

"I'm so sorry, honey. Jake emptied his backpack at my house last week and apparently a notice slipped under the couch. I know they probably sent a second flyer home, but I just wanted to be sure you knew about his early release."

The world around her seemed to come to a screeching halt.

"Today?"

"Yes, the teachers had some special workshop to attend."

Katy swallowed hard. "What time does school get out?"

"It let out at one o'clock."

"That was nearly two hours ago!"

"Oh, honey, I'm so sorry. I—I'm sure Jake took the bus home and is watching TV."

"Mom, I've got to call home."

"Okay."

Katy hit the speed dial button. The phone rang and rang, then finally went into voice mail.

She left a message telling Jake she'd be right there, just in case he'd been in the bathroom or totally engrossed in a video game. Then she grabbed her purse and keys and headed for the door, explaining to her boss on the way.

When Katy entered the apartment, she sighed in relief at the sight of Jake's backpack. He was home. She'd been frantic for nothing.

"Jake?" she called. No answer. And the TV was off. Not the norm when her son was home.

She glanced in his bedroom. It looked the same as when he'd left this morning—the bed slightly rumpled but basically tidy. The bathroom door stood open.

Panic threatened to return.

*Where could he be?*

What if someone had come to the door and Jake had let him in? He could be halfway to Mexico by now. Or worse.

"Calm down," she murmured. There was probably some reasonable explanation. No need to jump to conclusions. Jake was probably at a friend's house and had forgotten to call. It had happened once before. Fortunately, Brandon's mother had called that time to let her know Jake was there.

Katy removed her PalmPilot from her purse and ran through her address book. She called Brandon's house—no Jake. Now that she thought about it, Katy couldn't recall her son playing with Brandon recently.

Where could Jake be?

Her gaze lit on the bottle of wine, two-thirds gone, leftover from the dinner with Royce.

She grabbed her purse and headed out the door, taking the stairs because they were quicker. She was nearly out of breath when she reached Royce's door.

Katy pounded on the door a little harder than necessary. But he didn't answer. Her hand shook as she knocked one last time.

Should she call the police? Have them issue an Amber Alert?

Katy blinked away tears of frustration.


ROYCE CURSED under his breath as he chased the ball. "Sorry, kid, I don't catch so well one-handed."

"That's okay, I don't throw so good one-handed."

Royce picked up the ball and laughed. The sun was warm on his back and he recalled just how good it felt to be outdoors and playing. "I don't think of it that way. You're getting better, though."

"Yeah, so are you." Mischief lurked in Jake's eyes.

Royce tossed the ball to him and it bounced off the tip of his glove.

"Got to get under it."

"It was too high."

"Then move. Your feet aren't stuck to the ground." Royce demonstrated getting under the ball. Unfortunately, it bounced off his bare hand and he had to chase it again.

"It didn't help you."

"Yeah, well I'm the exception. Try it." He tossed the ball high.

Jake scampered back a few feet. He smiled as the ball fell into the pocket of his glove. "Cool. You got a trick like that for throwing?"

"Just keep focused on where you want it to go and follow through. Like this."

*"Jake Allan Garner."* The frosty words came from behind Royce.

Jake's eyes widened. He stammered, "Um, Mom, you weren't supposed to be home yet."

Royce turned to see Katy standing a few yards away, hands on hips, her eyes flashing.

"Why didn't you tell me there was early release today? Do you know how worried I've been?"

Jake opened his mouth, but Katy kept going. "I've called your friends, stopped by the school. I was about to call the police and have them issue an Amber Alert."

Royce stepped forward. "Didn't you get Jake's note?"

"There was no note." She enunciated clearly.

He turned. "Jake, you said you left a note."

The boy kicked a clod of dirt with his shoe. "I, um, forgot."

"It seems to me you deliberately disobeyed me. And pretty much orchestrated this whole thing. You knew I'd have Sally come stay with you for early release, didn't you?"

Jake studied his shoes. "I don't know."

"Yes, you do know. I'm beginning to think the notice got shoved under Grandma's couch on purpose. There's usually a second notice. I'm assuming that one got lost, too?"

The boy's face flushed. Royce had a pretty good idea Katy had hit the nail on the head.

"Hey, kid, it's not good going behind your mother's back." Royce turned to Katy. "I'm sorry, I should have known better."

She hesitated. "It's not your fault. He lied to you and will be punished." Crossing her arms, she turned to Jake. "You owe Royce an apology. Now."

"Sorry, Royce. I just wanted so bad for you to teach me." The longing in Jake's voice wounded him.

And reminded him of his son's pleas at about the same age. He'd always told himself Michael didn't need him that much. Maybe he'd been wrong.

But Jake presumably had a father. And Royce wasn't a good candidate to fill in even if the boy never saw his dad.

THE NEXT EVENING, Katy toyed with a hotel-issue pen while she phoned her mother. She'd landed in Chicago a few hours ago, but the ache of leaving Jake for several days was still fresh. Shaking her head, she was grateful her auction house only staged about ten out-of-town auctions each year. If she'd been with one of the larger houses, it might have been more.

Katy was about to hang up when her mother finally answered.

"Hi, Mom, how's it going?"

"Fine, dear. How was your flight?"

"Fine." No, it wasn't fine. But she wasn't about to admit it.

Come to think of it, her mother seemed a bit hesitant.

"Mom, are you sure everything's okay?"

"We can talk about it when you get home. It's about your arrangements with Sally. Nothing serious."

"Your tone says it *is* serious. Please tell me."

"I don't like to distract you from your work."

"Anything to do with Jake comes first. Tell me."

Her mother sighed. "Sally wasn't there today."

"When you picked up Jake? I know. She told me she was going to leave a little early."

"Sally never showed up."

Katy rubbed her temples. "Not at all?"

"No, but a strange man was there. Your neighbor, Royce?"

"Why was he there?"

"Apparently he and Jake have some sort of code...."

"Yes. Royce lives below us. They exchange Morse code messages through the floorboards."

"Are you sure that's wise, dear? I have to admit I'm a little surprised. You've always been very cautious where Jake is concerned."

"It's not like I planned it, Mom. And Royce seems to be a good man. Jake likes him."

"He's...a little rough around the edges."

"Why? Because he's missing a hand?"

Her mother made a noise of censure. "That's not what I meant."

"Look, Mom, Royce has government clearance, which includes an extensive background check. And I trust him." She was surprised to realize it was true.

"Well, I won't tell you how to raise your own child."

*Since when?*

Katy pushed away the disloyal thought. "I know you only want what's best for Jake."

"I just wish I'd been able to keep the house after your father died. There would have been plenty of room for you and Jake to move in."

Katy smiled at her mother's familiar refrain. "It probably wouldn't have been good in the long run. Besides, your condo is perfect for you."

"But I don't like Jake being alone like that. Who knows what might have happened before I got there."

The muscles on Katy's neck tightened. She could feel a headache starting along with the realization that some changes needed to be made. "There's not much I can do a thousand miles away. I'll handle it when I get home. Sally's all set to watch him after school tomorrow, isn't she?"

"That's just it. Her mother has a doctor's appointment. Jake will be all by himself unless I take time off work to pick him up.

I'm almost out of vacation time at the boutique."

Katy had rarely felt so helpless. It made her wonder, not for the first time, if she was being the kind of mother Jake deserved. But she simply couldn't see herself anywhere but in the world of car auctions.

"I don't want you to do that. You've already done so much for us." Katy hated owing anyone a favor, but the decision to spread the debt outside the family was especially difficult. "Maybe I can make other arrangements for the afternoon. Let me make a few phone calls and call you back."

"Other arrangements? I can take the time off without pay. No need to—"

"Yes, there is a need." She tried to infuse her voice with certainty. "I'll call you back. Bye, Mom."

ROYCE GROANED when the phone rang. He hoped it wasn't Becca doing her long-distance mother hen thing again.

"Hello." It came out sounding more irritable than he anticipated.

There was a hesitation, then, "It's Katy,

your upstairs neighbor. If this is a bad time, I can call later."

"No, it's fine. What can I do for you?"

"I'm in Chicago. Thank you for hanging out with Jake today. Apparently there was another babysitter miscommunication."

"No problem. The kid said he was hearing weird noises, so I went upstairs to check it out."

"We were lucky you were there. I owe you…about a year's supply of dinners."

Royce didn't like the anxiety in her voice. And he didn't like the fact that she seemed to think she owed him for such a little thing.

She hesitated. "I need to ask a favor."

"What kind of favor?"

"Would you mind, um, hanging out with Jake tomorrow after school? It's only for a couple hours and I'd be happy to pay you…."

Royce started pacing.

"Royce?"

"I'm here. Just checking my calendar."

More like stalling for time.

In the past, he would have avoided getting tangled up in Katy's problems. But that was before he woke up in a hospital room unable to recognize his own son because the kid had grown into a man when Royce wasn't looking. Though he'd failed Michael, maybe he could help Jake. It was only one day, after all.

"Um, yeah, I guess I can do it."

"You don't sound too sure. I really shouldn't have asked. It's no big deal, my mom can probably take time off work."

Clearing his throat, he said. "I'm sure. No big deal."

But it *was* a big deal. Anyone who knew him well would have been downright amazed.

## CHAPTER FIVE

ROYCE CHECKED the peephole before opening the door. "Mrs. Donovan, come in."

"I'm here for Jake."

"He'll be ready in a minute." He gestured awkwardly for her to enter, aware he was playing host in an apartment she probably knew as well as he did.

"Jake, it's your grandma. Get your bag," he called.

"Do I have to? I can stay here with you."

"Not for the weekend, buddy."

"Why not?"

"Because I said so." Wasn't that an appropriately parental way to dodge tough questions? "Now scoot."

"My bag's not packed yet."

"Why not?"

"You didn't tell me to."

Royce sighed. "You're ten years old, I shouldn't have to tell you."

Audrey Donovan stepped forward. "Jake, you know better."

"Hi, Grandma. I'll, um, go pack my bag."

The woman crossed her arms over her chest and eyed Royce as if he were an escapee from the penitentiary. "How long has my daughter known you?"

"About a month."

"She says you have some sort of government clearance."

"Yes, ma'am."

"I take it they check for felony convictions?"

"Among other things."

"I don't like Katy leaving Jake with someone inexperienced in child care. Do you know CPR?"

*Did he know CPR?* "Working in remote locations, I've even had to use it once or twice."

Royce didn't add that he'd flunked the baby Heimlich maneuver when Michael had been a toddler. He would never forget the panic in the baby's eyes as he'd struggled to breath. How helpless Royce had felt.

And how he'd done possibly the worst

thing—smacked Michael on the back hard enough to make the piece of hot dog fly out of his mouth. It could have just as easily lodged farther in his airway. After that, Royce had done everything in his power not to be left alone with Michael until way after he'd outgrown the choking stage.

Audrey's eyes narrowed, as if she could read his thoughts. She continued to question his capabilities until Jake came out with his duffel bag.

"I'm ready." His voice was glum.

"Why the long face?" Audrey asked.

"No reason. I just wanted to stay here with Royce. We played video games. You'd think he'd be really bad at it 'cause he only has one hand, but he's pretty good. And he was going to play catch with me."

"Time to go, Jake. You can see Royce… another time. I'll lock up, you can go ahead and leave."

Which he did, feeling as if he'd been dismissed in more ways than one.

ON MONDAY, Katy replaced the phone on the cradle and started to pace. What in the world was she going to do? Sally had called her at work and quit without notice.

She'd hurried home to be there when Jake arrived. Then, she'd called the nanny agency and been placed on a waiting list. Apparently several high-tech firms had opened offices in the valley, their new employees creating a shortage of private nannies, especially those willing to work part-time. The story was the same at the second and third agencies she called.

Katy started to panic. She would have called her friend Karen, but knew she was on vacation in Cancun.

Flipping open her laptop, Katy started to check listings for nanny services.

She heard the door open and Jake ran in the apartment. "Mom, you're home."

Glancing at her watch, she tried to smile. "Hi, honey, I...got off work early. How was your—"

"Look who I found downstairs."

Royce entered. His hair was windblown, his face tanned. It was good to see him looking so fit and healthy.

"Jake insisted I come upstairs with him.

For a snack. I figured I'd make sure Sally showed up."

"Thank you. That was very kind."

"No problem."

"I heard you on the phone with Grandma last night. About Sally taking so much time off."

"That's something I need to talk to you about, honey. Later."

Jake had grown attached to Sally and Katy didn't want to break the bad news with someone else here.

"I know Sally needs to be with her mom a lot." Jake's expression was earnest. "So I figured out a way she can do that."

"Sally called a while ago. She had to quit to take care of her mom." She held out her hand to him, determined to gloss over the very real challenges they faced. And the fact that Jake was losing another adult he'd come to count on. "I know it's going to be hard, but we'll get somebody new you like just as much as Sally."

"We don't need nobody new. We've got Royce."

"Royce is a welder, not a babysitter."

"He said he can't be a welder anymore, 'cause it takes two hands."

Katy couldn't allow Jake to put Royce on the spot any more than he already had. The man had been very patient. "It's out of the question, Jake. End of discussion. Now take your backpack to your room and start your homework."

"But—"

*"Now."*

"Yes, Mom." Jake slung his backpack over his shoulder and trudged to his room.

"Wow, you've got that threatening voice down pat. I was ready to salute."

"I've probably been too easy on him. Mostly because I understand that he's looking for a father figure. His dad's really dropped out of his life the past couple years. But I can't let him continue to put you on the spot. You've been great. Absolutely great."

Royce shifted. "So when will the new nanny start?"

"Good question. The agencies are having problems finding enough qualified people because of the high-tech boom. I'll figure something out, though."

*I always do.*

But this time, she had the feeling her luck had run out.

ROYCE STARED AT THE TV, but wasn't paying attention. He kept thinking about Katy and the flash of panic in her eyes when she'd talked about finding a new nanny. He remembered how she'd said it was extra hard finding someone qualified who would work part-time and weekends.

So why was he concerned? It wasn't his problem. Yet he couldn't help but feel a bit protective of Jake and Katy. He'd never gotten actively involved in his neighbors' business before, and that had been the beauty of being an expat. Royce could be as involved as he chose, because he knew he'd be moving on soon.

Royce resisted an idea begging to be explored. "No way. Not me."

*If not him, then who?* He'd learned that sentiment in one of his high school classes. Funny that it'd stuck with him all these years. Funnier still that he'd been able to ignore it. Until now.

Katy had said Jake was looking for a father figure. Royce had failed his own son, but maybe, just maybe, he could step in and make a difference for Jake, if only in the short term.

Royce grabbed his keys, locked the door and took the stairs to Katy's place. He knocked immediately, afraid he might change his mind. His idea was totally out of the norm for him, but somehow right.

Katy opened the door and motioned him inside. She was talking on the phone.

"Yes, I understand," she said. "There's no way you can find a replacement on such short notice. I'll be there Thursday evening as planned. But I'm going to need some comp time to spend with my son."

Her shoulders sagged as she clicked shut her phone. "Hi, Royce."

"Hi. Still no luck finding a nanny?"

"No. I've called everyone I can think of. I tried to get out of the show this weekend, but no luck. That's the problem working for a small house. I do several different jobs and can't be replaced on a moment's notice. We tend to have more auctions in the spring because the weather's good."

"Job security." He smiled to lighten her mood.

"That's one thing, I guess. Normally my mom could step in and take Jake for the weekend, but she's working mandatory overtime because of a big sale at the store."

"I might have a solution for you."

"Really? Have a seat." Katy gestured toward the couch and he complied. She sat in an easy chair.

Royce plunged in before he could have second thoughts. Or thirds. "Actually, it was Jake's idea. I'm not working right now and I can easily arrange my physical therapy around Jake's school schedule."

"I didn't think you'd seriously be interested."

"Only on a temporary basis, until you find another nanny. One who's qualified and all that."

Her shoulders straightened. "I'd pay you, of course."

He grinned. "Of course. I have to admit, I could use the cash until I get my disability claim worked out. My investments are long-term and I can't access my funds right now. But that's not the reason I suggested the plan. Jake's a great kid. I'd like to do it."

"It might just work. You're right here in the building. Jake likes you. I…trust you."

Royce loved seeing hope spark in her eyes. He felt good that he'd been the one to help put it there.

Katy placed her hand on his arm. His left arm, just below the elbow. "Are you sure you want to do this?" she asked.

Royce was mesmerized by the sight of her hand so close to his injury. He realized it was the first time anyone outside the medical profession had touched his damaged arm. It was a shock to find out how much he missed that contact.

"Positive." He'd never felt so sure of something in his life. And that scared him.

# CHAPTER SIX

WHEN THE PHONE RANG on Friday, Royce checked the caller ID display, half expecting it to read "unknown caller," the digital trick employed by some telemarketers.

Instead, it read "Garner, Katy."

"Hi, Katy. What's up?"

"I was just calling to see how it went yesterday."

"Fine. No problem. Jake's an easy kid to be around. As a matter of fact, he insisted on loading the dishwasher."

"Most of the time he's very good."

He thought he detected a smile in her voice.

"Most of the time? Now you've got me worried. Does he grow fangs during the full moon?"

Her chuckle was warm and made him smile.

She said, "I have the feeling this might be the honeymoon period."

"Honeymoon?"

"As in, he's on his best behavior because he doesn't want to scare you off."

"Hey, it takes a lot to scare me. I'm not totally unaccustomed to ten-year-old boys."

"Not much recent experience, though, huh?"

"It's coming back to me. Piece of cake."

If Saturday afternoon went just as well, he would be home free. Jake's grandmother would take him for the two nights and Royce would watch him during Audrey's Saturday shift at work. And Katy would be home Sunday. Not a bad arrangement as long as it was temporary.

"Good. I'll stop by with your pay Sunday night if I don't get in too late."

"Sounds good." Not only to have some much-needed cash, but to see Katy, too.

"HOW ABOUT WE PLAY some video games?" Jake asked, controller already in hand. "Since Grandma can't get here till seven."

"Just for a few minutes. We still need to

clean up our mess in the kitchen." He'd shown Jake how to make his own Rice Krispies Treats.

Both Friday and Saturday afternoons had gone surprisingly quickly. Royce idly wondered why he could spend time with Jake and enjoy himself, but hadn't been able to do the same with his own son without getting restless.

Royce suspected the answer was complex. As long as he thought of being responsible for Jake as a job, he didn't get that panicky, hemmed-in feeling he'd gotten during Michael's early years. He'd loved seeing the boy, but Royce's mind had quickly strayed to the next job, next adventure.

But it looked as if there might not be any new adventures for him.

Royce pushed away the thought. It would be too easy to lose hope completely. Picking up the second game controller, he proceeded to give Jake a run for his money.

"Royce?"

"Huh?"

"D'ya ever get scared?"

If only the kid knew. It was hard to

remember a time when he hadn't been scared. But he would guess it had been roughly seven months ago. "Yeah, sometimes."

"My mom gets scared. She tries not to show it, though."

"Like scared of spiders? Noises in the dark?"

"Nah. Like if people come to the door and she's not expecting them. Or weird things, birthday parties."

Royce chuckled as he maneuvered the joystick. "Okay, I have to admit, clowns kind of freak me out. Maybe I've seen too many bad horror flicks."

"Clowns make great bad guys. But it's not the clowns.... I've never been to a birthday party."

"Oh, come on. Not even one?"

Jake shook his head, his hand pausing on the controller. "Nope. I didn't used to get invited to them much. But now, I have a couple of friends. When I bring home an invitation, Mom gets this really weird look and makes an excuse why I can't go."

"Maybe it's just a coincidence."

"I don't think so." The boy's expression was so glum it made Royce hurt for him.

"Sometimes adults have reasons no one else understands."

"It's not fair."

"No, it isn't." He refrained from pointing out that a lot of things in life weren't fair. Such as having his hand blown to bits and losing everything.

"I got an invitation to my friend Chris's birthday party. He's gonna be eleven." Jake's expression brightened. "I bet you could talk my mom into letting me go. She likes you."

Even though it was an obvious snow job, Royce was flattered by the idea that Katy had a soft spot for him.

"You think?"

"Sure. You got a government clearance. And with only one hand, it's not like you could choke her or nothing."

Ah. His injury apparently made him non-threatening to women and children. Something he might consider using to his advantage in dating, if it didn't make him seem so damn pathetic.

"I guess you've got a point there."

"And you make her smile."

"I do?"

"Uh-huh. Will you talk to her about Chris's party?"

"It's not my place to butt in, kid." The whole situation smacked of getting involved. And the last thing he wanted was to get entangled in Jake's life on more than a short-term basis.

"You're my friend. And my mom's. I'd help you if you needed it."

The boy's logic was so straightforward and, well, noble, Royce found himself nodding in agreement. "Okay. But only if the subject comes up."

"What if it doesn't?"

"Then we'll know it wasn't meant to be."

KATY WAS RELIEVED when she saw the light shining beneath Royce's door. Good. She didn't want to wake him, but for some reason it seemed important that she pay him tonight.

Maybe the urgency came from the knowledge that he needed the money.

Who was she fooling? Katy simply wanted to talk to Royce, one adult to another. She'd been able to relax with Royce and found him easy to be around. Not her general experience with members of the opposite sex. Maybe that's why she'd married Eddie. They'd known each other since kindergarten, so she'd never had a hard time talking to him. Until they were married with Jake on the way and couldn't seem to stop fighting.

Katy knocked and heard rustling inside.

The door opened and Jake stood there, his shirt rumpled and his hair standing on end.

"I'm sorry, did I wake you? I saw your light on and thought it would be okay...."

"It's fine. I fell asleep on the couch." He rotated his shoulder. "Not a good idea."

"No, I guess not."

He stepped aside. "Come in."

"Just for a minute." Suddenly, she felt awkward about being on his doorstep.

"Have a seat." He ran his hand through his hair. "Oh, wait. You probably need to get right back to Jake."

She perched on the easy chair. "He's still at my mom's house. Since I'm so late, she offered to keep him tonight and take him to school tomorrow." Handing him the envelope, she said, "Here's your payment."

"Great, thanks." Royce tossed the envelope on an end table and sat on the couch.

"This arrangement seems to be working out. Jake is thrilled. You're all he talked about on the phone. How do you feel about it?"

Royce grinned, setting her at ease. "Better than I even anticipated. We had a good time."

"That's great. I was afraid you might have had enough. Kids can be wearing when you're not used to being around them twenty-four hours a day."

"They're definitely that. To be honest with you, Jake's a welcome distraction. I've had too much of my own company since I've been back in Phoenix." He leaned back. "Funny, when I was recovering at my sister's house, all the activity drove me nuts. I just wanted peace and quiet. But now that I have it, I'm a little lost."

"I know what you mean. My apartment seems really empty without Jake there. If my ex-husband insisted on his visitation rights, I'd probably be lost."

"He's not in the picture?"

"Not really. Eddie rarely asks to see him.

Just often enough to confuse Jake. And my dad died when Jake was a baby. It's mostly just me and my mom."

"You've done a great job with him."

His words meant more to her than he could ever know. She cleared her throat. "Thanks. I needed to hear that."

"It's the truth. I wasn't around much to notice what a terrific job my ex did until Michael was a grown man. Now I see how hard you work and I can appreciate Tess more."

"You, um, still have feelings for your ex?"

"Not the romantic kind. I admire her, admire what she's done with her life. And owe her big-time for pretty much raising our son."

"It takes a secure man to admit that. I don't know if Eddie will ever understand all he's missing. Maybe after the new baby is born… His girlfriend's pregnant."

"How's Jake taking it?"

"Better than I thought. Telling him was one of the hardest things to do. I owed it to Jake to be tactful and nonjudgmental when all I wanted was to say, 'Your daddy doesn't give a damn about you, but he's bringing another child into the world, anyway.'"

Royce shifted, glancing around the room.

Katy's face warmed. "I'm sorry, Royce. I've made you uncomfortable when all I wanted to do was thank you for being so great with Jake."

"No need to apologize. I'm just a little sensitive about the whole absentee dad issue." His posture remained stiff. "Though I'm paying for it now."

"How?"

"My son doesn't return my calls. My fault for not being the kind of involved father I should have been. It still stings, though."

"I'm sorry. I wouldn't wish that kind of hurt on anybody. At least you're trying now. Maybe he'll come around."

"Yeah, maybe."

"Well, you have a new fan, anyway. My mom's decided you might be okay. You won her over by teaching Jake to cook."

"Just Rice Krispies Treats."

"Still, she was impressed."

"So that's why she quit glaring daggers

at me. I still get the feeling she'd rather Sally was back."

"Not necessarily Sally. But another female would probably make her more comfortable."

"She doesn't see the importance of Jake having a guy for a role model?"

"She probably hasn't given it much thought. Though she knows my spending time with my dad was important. He taught me the value of hard work, showed me what was what under the hood of a car and encouraged me to be involved in the auction business."

"It is kind of an unusual occupation for a woman."

"It's been a man's world for so long. But there are more and more women involved in the actual auction itself. My dream is to be a bona fide auctioneer. There's something so exciting about being up there with all those people hanging on my every word, with things moving so fast most people can't keep up. It's such a rush."

"I wouldn't have you pegged as somebody who likes to be in front of an audience."

"That's just it. When I'm calling it's like I'm a whole different person. I'm good at the preauction administrative duties, but it's participating in the auction that I love most."

"No college?"

Katy shrugged. "A two-year degree. After that, all I wanted to do was join my dad and learn the business. When he died five years ago, I was glad I had that time working side by side with him. He was a gifted man."

"Sounds like it."

"How about you? Did you always want to be a welder?"

"No, I fell into it by chance. I was in community college and took a welding class as an elective, just to see what it was like. After that, I was hooked. There's something so organic about the process. It requires a special mind-set, a gift. And I have that gift." He frowned, scrubbing his hand across his face. "*Had* that gift."

For the first time, Katy clearly understood all he'd lost in the accident. Not only his hand and ability to do a lot of tasks, but also his identity.

Sadness washed over her as she searched

for words of encouragement. There were none. So she simply reached out and squeezed his hand.

The silence grew awkward.

"Well, I better get going."

Royce cleared his throat. "Thanks for the pay."

Katy strove to get back on safe ground. "I'll need you to work the same days next week, if that's okay?"

"Sure."

She made her way to the door, then stopped. "Jake said there was something you wanted to discuss with me?"

He frowned. "No. I wonder where he got—" Snapping his fingers he said, "I know what he's talking about. He wanted me to put in a good word so you'd let him go to his friend's birthday party."

Katy swallowed hard, unable to meet his gaze. "We don't do outside birthday parties."

"Is it a religious thing? I know there are faiths that don't celebrate birthdays."

"No." Though maybe she should have thought of joining one. It would have been easier than dodging an issue most people wouldn't understand, even though many had phobias of their own. Some people were terrified of flying, some hated heights. Katy got nauseous at the very thought of children's birthday parties. Though her reasons were logical in an illogical way, she was still embarrassed. And it wasn't as though she was going to share that part of her history with just anyone.

"We just don't."

"Okaay."

Glancing at her watch, she said, "Well, I've got to go."

Katy left, throwing "See you later" over her shoulder. Her hands were still shaking when she reached her apartment.

## CHAPTER SEVEN

ROYCE SHOOK HIS HEAD, staring at the door.
Katy had practically bolted.

The kid was right. She really was
spooked by birthday parties. And he
couldn't help but feel sorry for Jake. Maybe
Katy didn't realize birthday parties were
the glue that held the whole childhood
social scene together. Heck, even his dad
had managed to throw the occasional party
for Royce and Becca after their mom died.

Royce's gaze rested on the envelope Katy
had brought. Retrieving it from the end table,
he opened it. Nowhere near what he was accustomed to making, but satisfying all the
same. And enough to ease his money worries
until he knew where he stood with his disability and retraining.

Funny, everything seemed to be temporary these days. But then again, his life had always been that way. The only difference was that impermanence no longer satisfied him. He needed something to hold on to after all the drastic changes in his life.

And the nanny gig, temporary though it was, seemed likely to supply him with that. Who'd have thought?

A FEW WEEKS LATER, Jake watched Katy place the receiver on the cradle and sigh. Rubbing her head as if she had a headache.

"What's wrong, Mom?" he asked.

"Oh, nothing really. My boss recommended me to a nonprofit group that's conducting a charity auction before the real auction this weekend. I had to tell them no."

"How come?"

She ruffled his hair. "Because it would mean more time away from you. My out-of-town assignments seem to be increasing bit by bit. If I don't watch it, I'll be away from home all the time. I can't allow that to happen—you mean too much to me. And it's not going to pay much since it's for charity."

Jake thought about that. Sometimes it made him sad when his mom was gone, but being with Royce made it better. "It's okay for you to be gone more now that I'm getting bigger. I bet you'd get a tax deduction, too. I've seen the H&R Block commercials."

His mother smiled. "I suppose you're right. It *is* for a good cause. And it would be good PR."

"What's that?"

"Public Relations. Get me more exposure, more clients. Who knows, it might even be televised."

"That would be totally cool, Mom." He went and gave her a hug. "I bet Royce could watch me. Maybe even invite me to sleep over."

She hugged him tight. "You're a good boy, you know it? But I'm not sure about a sleepover…."

"Royce is one of the good guys, Mom. You don't need to worry. And that way Grandma won't get tired of having me too many days."

"You're sure you're okay with me being gone that long?"

Jake nodded.

It wasn't a lie. He really did want to do guy stuff with Royce. He also wanted something else so bad he could taste it—he wanted to go to his first-ever birthday party. The way the kids described it, parties were almost as good as Christmas and Easter rolled into one.

He practically held his breath as his mom picked up the phone and punched in the numbers. She talked to Royce and he must've said okay, because she kept thanking him. Jake hoped Royce had agreed because he liked Jake and not because his mom had offered to pay extra.

When his mom was on the phone to change her flight, he went into the kitchen and got the party invitation from the message board on the refrigerator. He always put invitations there, hoping his mom would relent.

She never did.

Jake closed his eyes, crossed his fingers and prayed that Royce would come through for him.

THERE WAS A KNOCK at Royce's door promptly at 3:45 on Thursday. He opened the door, trying not to be nervous about playing Mr. Mom for a couple nights. "Hi, Jake. You got your stuff?"

"Yep. It's all here." He patted his duffel bag, avoiding Royce's gaze. "I gotta do my homework right off."

"Wow, you're pretty eager today."

Jake shrugged, dropped his bag on the floor and headed to the breakfast bar with his backpack.

This was going to be easier than Royce had thought. Jake seemed intent on taking care of himself.

"How was your day?" Royce asked.

"Good."

"Anything interesting happen?"

The kid didn't even look up from his math workbook. "Nope."

Giving up, Royce turned on the TV.

Then Jake glanced up and sighed. "I'm trying to do homework here."

"Oh. Sorry." Royce clicked the Off button.

Silence descended, with the exception of Jake's pencil scratching across the page.

Royce was relieved when the phone rang some time later. He nearly pounced on the handset. "Hey."

"What's up, big brother?"

"Nothing much." .

Jake glanced up from his homework. "Is that my mom?"

"No, it isn't," Royce whispered.

"Oh." Jake's shoulders relaxed and he went back to his fractions.

"Who're you talking to?" his sister demanded, always the interrogator.

"Just Jake."

"Who's Just Jake?"

"Jake Garner. A neighbor."

"He sounds like a child."

"Because he *is* a child."

"And he's with you because…"

Royce closed his eyes, willing this conversation away. He didn't want Becca getting caught up in the details of his life because she'd try to micromanage him for sure.

"Because I'm watching him as a favor to a friend."

Jake eyed him with interest.

Becca went in for the kill. "A female friend?"

"Yes. Strictly platonic."

She chuckled. "Royce, you haven't had a

platonic female friend since the eighth grade."

"There's a first time for everything. I'm not quite the catch I used to be, in case you haven't noticed."

"What's there to notice?"

"The gray around my temples. A few laugh lines. A missing hand. Things that tend to keep the young hotties away."

"Then maybe you better set your sights on women your own age."

"Hey, I've dated a few of those."

"Good, I'm glad to hear you're maturing."

"Thanks for the vote of confidence."

Sighing, she said, "You know I only want you to be happy, don't you?"

"Yeah, I know. Otherwise I wouldn't put up with you."

Jake stood in front of him, waiting expectantly.

"I'm on the phone, buddy," Royce whispered.

"It's time to go."

Royce covered the mouthpiece. "Go where?"

"The party."

"Your mom said you don't do parties."

Jake raised his chin. "She changed her mind."

"Royce, are you there?"

"Hey, Becca, I gotta go. I'll talk to ya later."

"But—"

"Bye." He replaced the receiver on the cradle, directing all his attention to the boy. "What gives?"

"My mom changed her mind." He couldn't quite meet Royce's eyes.

"I guess I better just call her and confirm."

"She's in the air. Can't take calls."

Royce had the feeling he was being played. "Then I guess that means no party."

Jake's eyes widened. "You really won't… let me go?"

The quiver in the kid's voice got to Royce. Would it really matter if he took Jake to the party and it turned out Katy hadn't expressly agreed? Every child should experience a birthday party with his friends.

For the sake of argument, Royce asked, "What about a present?"

"I've got a card I made and put some money inside. He'll like that."

Royce nodded slowly. "I bet he will. Where'd you get the money?"

"From my bank. It's left over from Christmas."

"Your mom let you use your own money?"

"Yeah." Jake hesitated. "She said it would, um, build character."

Royce ran his hand over his jaw to hide a smile. His throat got kind of scratchy at the same time. The kid wanted this so bad he was willing to use his meager savings.

"It appears she was right. Do you have the invitation with you? Can we walk?"

"Yep." Jake pulled a dog-eared invitation from his pocket, the print smudged from much handling. "Two streets over, across from Desert Arroyo Park. I'll show you."

"I guess you will."

Royce grinned as Jake let out a whoop. The boy deserved a little fun.

KATY CALLED HOME out of habit when she arrived at the hotel. No answer. Then she remembered Jake was probably at Royce's place.

She fidgeted while Royce's cell rang, muttering a curse when it went to voice mail. She disconnected without leaving a message.

He picked up the third time she called. It sounded as if he was in the middle of a war zone. Lots of screaming and banging.

"Royce? It's me, Katy."

"Oh, um, hi. Let me go outside where it's quieter."

She heard a door slide and the background noise dropped considerably.

"What was all that about?"

"Um, festivities."

"You're throwing a party while you're supposed to be watching my son?"

"I'm not the one throwing the party."

"What's going on? I want to talk to Jake."

"He can't come to the phone right now."

Katy was tired and crabby and wanted to talk to her son. "Why not?"

"Because he's blindfolded and swinging a stick."

"Royce, this is really—"

"Look, I gotta go. He just busted that thing wide-open. I'll call you when we get home."

Tears of frustration gathered. She stared at her phone, willing Royce back.

The birthday party.

Dread settled in her stomach. Katy tried to tell herself that she had nothing to worry about. What could possibly happen when Royce was there to watch over Jake?

But the fear remained.

# CHAPTER EIGHT

ROYCE SPREAD THE BLANKET over Jake, tucking it under his chin. The kid was exhausted. But even in sleep, a smile curved his punch-stained lips.

It made Royce's chest ache with emotion he didn't want to define.

Squaring his shoulders, he prepared himself for a difficult explanation. He grabbed the phone and went into his bedroom, closing the door behind him.

"Hey, Katy, it's Royce."

"Where have you been? I've been calling for hours."

"I told you I'd call when we got home. I had to get Jake settled in on the couch. The kid was ready to drop."

"Is he okay?" The hint of panic in her

voice bothered him. Surely she knew he could handle this?

Then again, Royce hadn't been so sure himself. He wasn't used to being the one keeping the home fires burning.

"Of course he's okay. Maybe a little too much ice cream and cake, but one satisfied ten-year-old."

"That's just great. You took my son to a birthday party against my wishes and allow him to gorge himself on sugar. What else do you have in your if-it-feels-good-do-it arsenal?"

Royce was surprised by her attack. "You're out of line, Katy. I apologize for taking Jake to the party when he didn't have your permission. For the record, he told me you'd changed your mind."

"And you believed him? You could have called."

"You were in the air. If you ask me, I'm not the one you should be angry with."

"Believe me, Jake will be punished. I— I'm sorry for overreacting."

"What's this all about?"

"It's nothing you'd understand."

"Try me," he murmured.

"I…can't. I've got to go, Royce. I'll talk to you when I get home. Bye."

The line went dead and Royce was left staring at the phone. There was something going on with Katy. If she was in trouble, he wanted to know.

Shaking his head, he tried to regain some of his usual detachment. Katy was able to handle her own problems. Besides, he made a very unlikely knight in shining armor.

KATY HESITATED outside Royce's door on Sunday evening. She was about to leave when the door opened and he stood there, trash bag in hand.

"Hey, Katy, come on in. I can take this out later."

"I can't stay long, I'm on my way to pick up Jake from my mother's house. I just wanted to drop off your pay." She handed him the envelope. "And talk about what happened while I was gone."

He set down the trash bag and gestured for her to follow him. "Sure. There's some stuff Jake left here, too."

She hesitated in the doorway. "I'm sorry I overreacted the other night. But you have to trust my judgment where Jake's welfare is concerned."

Royce picked up Jake's shoes and backpack, his movements strained. "Taking him to a birthday party was hardly endangering his welfare."

"And how do you know that?" How could she explain in a way that wouldn't make her sound nuts? She couldn't and that frustrated her. "It's not like you understand the challenges of raising a child."

Hurt flashed in Royce's eyes.

Stepping forward, she said, "I'm sorry, Royce. I'm out of line again. I meant you don't know what raising a child is like today. Your son is grown."

"I got your meaning loud and clear the first time. I've made some mistakes in the past and I pay for them every time I see Michael on TV and think the sportscasters know him better than I do. Every time I leave a voice message and don't get a return call. But you know what bothers me most about you making this about me?" His anger seemed to evaporate. "It's that you don't trust me enough to tell me the truth about what's going on. I thought we were friends."

His admission surprised her. And forced her to look at him differently. Somehow friendship had crept in when she least expected it.

Katy touched his arm. "I *do* trust you. But it's something I'm not comfortable discussing right now. Will you accept that?"

He held her gaze. His voice was husky when he said, "I guess I will."

SWEAT DRIPPED off Royce's face as he did one more set of curls.

"You're like a man possessed today," Gus commented, winking. "It's gotta be a woman."

"Yeah, but not in the way you think." Royce gritted his teeth, working through the pain. "You really think this will help with my recovery?"

"You bet. But even if it doesn't, you'll work some nasty resentments out of your system."

Royce smirked. "You're a *physical* therapist, Gus, not a shrink. Give it a rest."

"What's the matter, I hit the nail on the head?"

Grunting, Royce refused to give him the satisfaction of knowing he was right.

"I told you you'd be back in the saddle again before you knew it. Chicks don't mind a guy missing appendages as long as he's still got the one that counts." Gus chortled at his own bad joke. "What's her name?"

"It's not like that. She's my employer and her name is Katy."

Gus opened his mouth, probably to zing in one more salacious joke.

Royce glared at him, the same glare that had stopped several bar fights before a punch had been thrown. Living in countries where he didn't always speak the language fluently had made him develop nonverbal cues necessary to survive.

Gus shook his head, raising his hands in defeat. "You don't want to talk about it, fine with me. You seriously need to lighten up, man. We're done for today. And the occupational therapist says you've made a lot of progress. Looks like she wants to give you an aptitude test next."

"I guess." Grabbing a towel, Royce wiped the perspiration from his face and the back of his neck. Tossing it on the bench, he picked up the weight and replaced it on the rack. "One thing I can't get used to is everything taking so long. Even getting dressed is a chore. There's no such thing as multitasking with one hand."

"Sure there is. You just gotta be more creative. And if that doesn't work, a prosthesis will help."

"You talk about that thing like it's the Holy Grail. I'm still not sure I want to go that route."

Gus clapped him on the shoulder. "That's something only you can decide. I've seen people thrive with and without. It's all in your attitude."

"Thriving is good. I could even live with competent. My employer seems to think I'm not capable of taking care of her kid. Like one ten-year-old is going to get the best of me."

"Because of your injury?"

"No." He explained the whole birthday party fiasco. "I still don't understand why she got so ticked off. She says she trusts me."

"Sounds like her issues, not yours."

Exactly. So why did it seem as if her issues had become his?

"You know, Gus, if you ever get tired of breaking my balls with physical therapy, you might just have a shot at that whole psychology thing."

"Not on your life." Gus started for the door. As an afterthought, he turned and said, "Oh, and one thing you might want to consider. Why is it so important what this woman thinks? You told me it's only a temporary gig."

Royce cursed under his breath.

And cursed again when he thought he heard Gus chuckle. The man was either a genius or one sadistic SOB.


ROYCE HELD HIS BREATH while he waited for the tone. He'd already left a couple messages for Michael and this was getting downright pathetic. But he couldn't seem to help himself. The explosion, horrible as it had been, had brought things into focus for him. Made him slow down long enough to figure things out. And wonder about the course of his life.

"Hi, Dad. Sorry I didn't get back to you, but my schedule's been really crazy."

It took a few moments for Royce to realize there was a living, breathing human being on the other end of the line.

He cleared his throat. "No problem, kid. I know how hectic your life is. I just wanted you to know I was thinking about you."

"That's great. I've been thinking of you, too."

The lie made Royce sad, mostly because he knew his son had learned it from him.

"You did great in the race Sunday."

"You saw it?"

"Sure did. I watch all your races."

"Cool. It was a tough one, but I managed third place. I think we're getting the bugs worked out of my new ride."

"That's terrific."

Then there was silence.

Royce cleared his throat. "Um, I was thinking maybe we could get together next time you race out West. I could fly to meet up with you."

"Yeah, maybe we can do that sometime. I gotta run, Dad. Talk to ya later."

"Yeah, bye."

But he was talking to dead air. Michael had already hung up.

Royce leaned back in his chair and squeezed his eyes shut. He'd expected Michael to be as eager as he to forge a relationship. Instead, his son didn't seem to care.

Was he too late?

## CHAPTER NINE

ROYCE HAD PUSHED the phone call with Michael to the back of his mind by Thursday, when he walked home from the bus stop after a grueling physical therapy session.

As he began to whistle, Royce realized he was looking forward to watching Jake today. Probably because Jake seemed to have a case of hero worship and was always happy to see Royce. Unlike Michael.

Purpose propelled Royce's steps. He had to get home and showered before Jake arrived. Which he managed to accomplish with just minutes to spare.

His hair still wet, he opened the door at Jake's knock and grabbed his keys. He and Katy had agreed that it was best for him to watch Jake at Katy's place on weekdays. "Hey, kid, how was your day?"

"Okay." His glum answer surprised Royce.

"I thought you were getting your state for that report today. Don't tell me, you got New Jersey." Royce locked the door and they headed toward the elevator.

"I got Oregon. It's an okay state."

"Not bad."

Once inside, Jake stabbed the button for the fourth floor. "Sunday is the father-son picnic for my Scout troop."

"Does your mom know?"

"Nah, I forgot to tell her."

"Really forgot? Or is this another smoke screen?"

Jake glared at him. "No. What's a smoke screen, anyway?"

"It was a way of asking if you were lying like you did about the birthday party. Your mom was pretty ticked off at both of us. I don't want to be the kind of guy she can't trust. Do you?"

"I'm *not* lying." He frowned. "My mom would let me go if my dad took me. But he never does stuff like that."

"Maybe we should call your mom when

she gets to her hotel. She might be able to call your dad and see." Royce found himself thinking Katy's out-of-town weekends were a little more frequent than she'd initially indicated. But this weekend, she was filling in for a coworker who'd had knee surgery.

"Won't do any good."

Royce rested his hand on Jake's shoulder. "Maybe, maybe not. But you should at least talk to your mom, find out what she thinks."

"She won't come out and say my dad doesn't care enough to go. But that's what it means."

Royce felt way out of his depth. The irony of the situation didn't escape him.

"I don't know what to tell you…. I missed out on a lot of my son's stuff when he was your age. Sometimes there was a good reason, like I was working on the other side of the world. Sometimes I was just…selfish."

Jake unlocked the door and Royce followed him into the apartment.

The kid's eyes narrowed and he looked older than he should. "Selfish is just another way of saying you didn't care. I feel sorry for your son."

Royce tried not to flinch. "He turned out okay."

"That's what he tells you. But I bet he isn't okay."

"Hey, I don't need to explain myself to a ten-year-old. Michael grew up just fine. He's a race-car driver. They don't let everyone do that."

"Even race-car drivers like to go to picnics." His logic was simple, yet totally decimating.

Royce ran a hand through his hair. "I screwed up, okay? And it's something I really regret and I'm trying to make up for. Now, you need to get started on that homework and we'll call your mom in a while."

"Whatever."

"Yeah, whatever."

And here Royce had thought the kid hero-worshiped him, when apparently he was simply a reminder of his no-good, lazy father.

Royce found this whole father-son dynamic confusing. Even if Jake wasn't his real son. Maybe he just wasn't cut out for this.

KATY'S CELL RANG a few minutes after she landed. Tired and with a scratchy throat giving her fair warning she was getting a cold, she sighed.

"Yes, Royce, what is it?"

"Jake says the father-son picnic for his Scout troop is this weekend. He seems pretty bummed out about missing it."

She stifled a groan. "I should have known it was coming up. It's always hard on Jake. I took him last year so he wouldn't miss out, but it's just not the same as having his dad there."

"The picnic is on Sunday. Any chance your ex would take Jake if he knows how important it is?"

"Probably not. Eddie told me to quit asking, said I was trying to guilt him into doing things with Jake. How fair is it to disappoint a little boy? Maybe he *should* feel guilty."

"Okay, so Eddie's not an option. Any chance you can come back early on Sunday?"

"What time does it start?"

"Ten in the morning."

"Even if I caught the first flight Sunday morning, I wouldn't be there in time." Katy knew her voice was starting to rise. But dammit, she felt so helpless. "I've always wanted more for Jake. A mom, a dad and everything that goes with it. It just seems like there isn't enough of me to go around."

Royce's voice sounded husky when he said, "I know, Katy. It sucks. I guess I never realized how much the everyday stuff means to a kid. But Jake knows you love him and do your very best for him."

"Some days, my best just isn't good enough. I imagine what he wants more than anything right now is to go to that picnic."

"Yeah, pretty much."

"Would you put him on the phone?"

"Sure, hold on a sec."

There was a delay as they handed off the phone.

"Hi, Mom."

At hearing his voice, a wave of homesickness hit her so hard her eyes burned. "Hi, sweetie. I'm sorry about the picnic. I won't be home in time to take you."

"No big deal."

"It *is* a big deal. You don't know how much I wish things were different."

"Me, too. I, um, got Oregon for my state project."

"Very cool."

They chatted more about Jake's day and then he put Royce back on the line.

"Hey, Katy, I've got an idea."

"What's that?"

"How about if I take Jake to the picnic? Would that make you uncomfortable?"

"Not at all, but it's not necessary. That's way beyond the call of duty."

"I want to do it. I wasn't there for Michael with this kind of stuff and I'd really like to be there for Jake on Sunday."

Katy tucked her hair behind her ear. "Are you sure?"

"Very. I would have suggested it sooner but I was worried you might not trust me enough. You know, after the birthday party."

"It was never a matter of trusting you, it's everyone else I don't trust. The picnic is fine, though." She didn't want to examine why that was true. "If I get in early enough, I may be able to meet you guys over there. Is it at Desert Arroyo Park like last year?"

"Yep."

"I'll try to make it before the end." She hesitated. "And Royce, thanks."

"You're welcome." The warmth in his voice stayed with her long after the call was over. And the reassurance that, at least for a little while, she had someone to help carry the parental load. It was an unexpected blessing.

KATY MADE IT TO THE PARK shortly after noon, but couldn't find a parking space close to the picnic. There were fathers and sons all over the place, as well as women streaming in to catch the last event of the day. How in the world would she find Jake and Royce?

She followed the sound of cheering and, happily enough, was in time to see them tie their legs together for the three-legged race.

She was unable to catch Jake's eye, but she enjoyed the chance to watch Jake and Royce together when they didn't know she was there. Jake's grin was broad and Royce's smile was almost as wide. They were obviously enjoying themselves. That made her feel somewhat better about not having been there from the beginning.

Royce wrapped his left arm around Jake's shoulder, Jake twined his right arm around Royce's waist and they made their way to the starting line.

Katy's throat got scratchy and not from the cold she was keeping at bay. This time it was from the admiration shining in Jake's eyes as he glanced up at Royce for guidance. And she ached for Royce, whom she suspected must be painfully aware this was the only circumstance in which he would ever again have two hands. It made her angry at fate. And sad for what both guys were missing. And very, very happy that they had this moment together.

"They should give that one guy a head start," the mother behind her commented to a friend.

"So sad. I wonder how he lost his hand? Maybe he was in Iraq."

Their curiosity sounded wrong to Katy. It sounded as if they thought Royce should be the object of pity, yet he was the most together man she'd met in a long, long time.

Katy gave the two women a pointed look. "He's my friend and he does just fine."

The women murmured an apology and moved off.

A big guy with salt-and-pepper hair ambled over. "People make wrong assumptions sometimes."

Katy shifted, smiling slightly. "Yes, but I felt I had to say something. That's my son out there racing with him."

The man nodded and turned his attention to the field as the starting gun went off.

Katy forgot about him as she watched the awkward gait that came from Royce and Jake trying to work as one. She cried out as Jake stumbled, but Royce quickly pulled him upright, his forearm wedged beneath Jake's armpit.

He flinched in pain, but kept moving toward the finish. It was a dead heat between two teams.

By the time Jake and Royce crossed the finish line, Katy was jumping up and down, screaming.

"Jake. Royce," she called and waved.

They turned in unison toward her voice.

Both had huge victory grins. But she got the feeling they'd found something special that had nothing to do with winning. For a short while, neither had focused on what he'd lost. Only what he'd gained.

They hobbled over to her, still tied together.

"Mom, when did you get here? Did you see the whole race? We won!"

"I got here right before it started. You guys are the best!"

"We did pretty good, didn't we, Royce?"

A look passed between the two, significant yet indefinable. As if they shared a secret.

Katy swallowed hard. Secrets weren't good. She shook off the uneasiness and instead looped her arm over Jake's shoulder, resting her hand against the warm solidity of Royce's biceps.

"You two were terrific!"

Royce tilted his head. "We *were* pretty terrific, weren't we?"

The big guy with the salt-and-pepper hair came over. "Hey, Royce, I told you those curls would come in handy."

Royce clasped the man's hand. "Gus, what're you doing here?"

"Came to watch my brother and nephew. You left 'em in the dust."

"Katy, this is my physical therapist, Gus."

She shook his hand, too, all the while trying to recall if she'd said anything that might be misconstrued. "I've heard a lot about you."

"None of it good, I hope. If Royce liked me too much, it would mean I wasn't doing my job." His eyes twinkled with amusement. "I've heard a lot about you, too, all of it good."

Katy glanced at Royce, who looked as if he wanted to wring Gus's neck. From what she'd heard of the physical therapist, he'd probably tell Royce to go ahead and try—good therapy and all that.

She wanted to ask what Royce had said about her. Then a horrible realization hit. With all her cheering, Gus might have gotten the wrong impression about her relationship with Royce.

Sure enough, Gus's knowing look told her he had put two and two together and arrived at five.

"Royce is, um, my son's nanny."

"Uh-huh." Gus winked, as if Royce might be fulfilling more personal duties. "Nanny."

Her face warmed at the thought. Not so much because it was off base, but because it was, well, interesting to contemplate.

Not for the first time, Katy cursed Sally for being so unreliable and getting her into this.

Royce leaned close. "Aren't there other titles I could have? Like Kid Wrangler or VP of Afterschool Activities? Nanny reminds me of some British woman." He shuddered.

Katy laughed. "You're no Mary Poppins or Supernanny. So you can use whichever title you prefer." She tilted her head, studying him. "Kid Wrangler suits you."

"Kid Wrangler it is."

Gus shook his head and slapped Royce on the back. "I'll leave you to your…duties. Nice to meet you, Katy."

He had the nerve to chuckle as he sauntered away.

"Is he always that annoying?" she asked.

"Always. But he has heart."

Katy thought the description fit Royce better than Gus. Yes, Royce definitely had heart.

## CHAPTER TEN

KATY'S MOUTH WATERED as she approached her apartment. She fervently hoped the terrific aroma was coming from her place.

Opening the door, she was greeted by an eager ten-year-old boy and the welcome sight of Royce working in her kitchen, a towel tucked at the waist of his jeans instead of an apron.

"Hi, honey." She hugged Jake.

"We're makin' dinner, Mom."

"I can see that. What a nice surprise."

"Yeah, Royce is doing the lasagna and I'm in charge of the garlic bread."

She ruffled his hair. "An important job."

"Yep, Royce says so."

Katy dropped her purse on the counter and went into the kitchen, where she peeked inside the oven. "Smells heavenly."

Royce grinned. "Yeah, I make a mean Italian meal."

"Family recipe?"

"In a way. The single father's defense kit. This is my dad's recipe."

"How cool. I see you found my food processor."

"Yep. My occupational therapist says I just have to work smarter and find the right tools."

"She's obviously right. And Jake and I benefit. Your dad cooked from scratch? I'm impressed."

"It kind of embarrassed me as a kid. The rest of the kids had a mom to do that. I'm beginning to understand what a great job he did."

"Royce, am I doing this right?" Jake asked.

Katy smothered a smile. He had as much garlic butter on his fingers as on the sourdough bread.

"Perfect." Royce gave him a thumbs-up.

Jake returned to his task, his tongue sticking out slightly in concentration.

She removed a glass from the cupboard

and filled it from the iced tea pitcher in the refrigerator. "Your father sounds like a phenomenal man."

"He is. Though I didn't appreciate it until recently. It hadn't even computed that Dad put his life on hold for us. I just figured that's what all parents did."

Katy turned her head so Royce couldn't see the emotion in her eyes. Clearing her throat, she said, "No, not all parents."

"Yeah, well I sure didn't live up to his example…." There was a trace of pain in his voice. "He remarried a couple years back and moved to Florida. I'm glad he's found a second shot at love—he deserves it. Maybe I ought to tell him that sometime."

Glancing up, Katy was surprised to find that Royce was watching her intently. "I bet he'd like that," she said.

Royce nodded. "Maybe."

"Am I done now?" Jake asked.

"You sure are." Royce wrapped the bread in aluminum foil. Opening the oven by wedging his left forearm through the handle, he slid the foil packet next to the lasagna pan. Turning to Jake, he said, "Good job, kid."

"Can I go play video games?"

Katy opened her mouth to respond, but Royce beat her to the punch. "You finished your homework?"

"All of it."

"Okay."

Jake went into the other room.

"You handled that like a pro," Katy observed.

Royce grinned. "Thanks. The question or the garlic bread?"

"Both. Your occupational therapy seems to really be working."

"They've given me some good tips. And my wound isn't as sensitive since Gus has been working me so hard."

"You're a natural with Jake. I have a hard time imagining you as anything but a hands-on kind of father." She retrieved an antibacterial cloth from the container under the sink and slowly wiped down the counter. "Have you reached Michael yet?"

"Yeah, he picked up his phone the other day."

"And?"

"And he doesn't seem to want to see me. I

offered to fly to meet him when he races out here again. He kind of blew off the suggestion."

"Have you ever told him how sorry you are?"

"That's something I can't say over the phone. I figured I'd tell him when we're face-to-face."

Katy tried hard not to paint Royce and her ex-husband with the same brush. It was difficult, though, especially remembering how many times Jake had been hurt by Eddie's thoughtlessness. "If he was disappointed a lot, he may be waiting to make sure you're sincere."

"It's a catch-22, then. How can I prove I'm sincere, if he won't see me?"

"Keep at it. Don't give up. You may have to fight to regain his trust."

"How long do I keep at it before I have to admit he's just not interested? I'm starting to feel like some pathetic stalker."

Shrugging, Katy said, "As long as it takes."

"Why can't we just start new?" There was a note of frustration in Royce's voice as he dropped dirty utensils in the sink. "I'm sorry, really, really sorry and I'm willing to tell him that. What more does he want?"

"To test you? To make sure you want a relationship badly enough to fight for it? Maybe even to punish you a little?"

He hesitated. "It sounds like you've thought about this."

"I have. I wonder if Eddie will ever realize how much he's missed. I wonder how Jake will handle it if Eddie decides he wants to have a relationship, especially if a lot of time has passed." She tossed the wipe in the trash. "And I wonder how I'll handle it."

"You'd be happy for Jake, though, wouldn't you?"

She had a hard time meeting his gaze. "I'd want to be. But I'd also wonder if Eddie was just setting him up for an even bigger letdown. And I imagine I'd resent the hell out of him even if he was sincere."

"I guess I never thought of it that way."

"Have you talked to your ex-wife about it?"

He shook his head. "No, Tess has enough on her hands with a new husband and new adopted daughter. She doesn't need me rehashing this old stuff. Besides, Michael's a grown man. We should be able to handle this without involving his mother."

"It was just a thought. Even grown men value their mother's opinion. At least I hope Jake will." Just as she hoped Royce would be able to reconcile with his son. Because he'd shown her he was a caring, stand-up guy. Michael McIntyre could do a lot worse for a father.

ROYCE TAPPED HIS PENCIL on the breakfast bar, eyeing the aptitude test results as if they were a snake. What if it was totally lame? What if it said he was good for absolutely nothing? Or worse yet, spouted platitudes about how he could be anything he wanted as long as he wanted it badly enough.

Royce mentally cursed his occupational therapist for insisting he take the stupid test. Then he flipped over the cover sheet and started reading. He hadn't gotten far when a knock sounded at his door. It was Katy.

"Hey," he said, taking in her tousled hair and snug jeans. When he'd first met her, she'd been merely cute. Now cute bordered on irresistible.

"Hey." Her smile was shy, as if she knew exactly what he was thinking. This new facet of their friendship was unsettling to say the least. And…interesting.

"What's up? Want to come in?"

"No. Jake and I are going out for an ice cream and he thought you might want to come with us."

"Sure, sounds great. Where is the kid?"

"Putting the finishing touches on his Oregon report. He should be done by the time we get up to my place. That's the reason for the ice cream—we're celebrating."

"Come on in while I get some shoes and my wallet."

She followed him inside, glancing at his bare feet. "Shoes you'll need, but the ice cream is my treat."

He flashed a grin. "I love a woman who buys."

"If things work out, I might be able to do it more often."

"How's that?"

"A headhunter called today. He was impressed by my work at that televised charity auction. Apparently he has at least one client who might be looking for a ringman. I told him the Parkers have been good to me and I'm not interested in a lateral move. That's when he said his client might be willing to offer auctioneer training. And he hinted the job was at one of the big houses."

"That's great. You work hard and deserve to move up. I've never seen you work an auction, but I bet you're great."

"Thanks. It's what I've always dreamed of. I'd planned on going to auctioneering school after community college, but I went straight into the business instead. I absolutely *know* I could be good at calling if I practiced enough. As it is, I only get to call in short spurts to relieve the regular auctioneers. Finally, someone is talking about training me."

"They won't do that where you're at?"

"The Parkers are nice people and they've been really good to me. But it's a family business and only family gets groomed to call."

He leaned over and hugged her in encouragement. "Then I hope this pans out for you. So the ice cream is a double celebration?"

"No, Jake doesn't know yet. And I don't want him to unless it's a sure deal."

"Congratulations."

"Thanks." Katy glanced at the papers on the breakfast bar.

"Aptitude test results," he explained.

She smiled sheepishly. "It's none of my business. You probably think I'm the nosiest human being alive."

"Nah. I'd like to think it's because we're friends and you care about your friends."

She nodded slowly. "Of course. You've got your wallet?"

Royce grinned. "I thought I didn't need my wallet? You're buying."

"I, um, you're right."

He'd flustered her. And for some reason, that made him happy. Because it meant she wasn't immune to him as a man. Hadn't delegated him to the asexual cripple category.

Whistling quietly, he closed and locked his door.

His temporary nanny gig was turning into a lot more than he'd anticipated.

JAKE WATCHED HIS MOM eat her ice cream. She was pretty, or at least his friends said so. They also said she was probably doing the big nasty with Royce.

He didn't think so. Royce never spent the night and they didn't touch and kiss. Well, they touched sometimes, but not *that* way.

Besides, his friend Chris had pretty much become obsessed with the big nasty since he'd walked in on his dad and mom.

Personally, Jake figured his mom had never had sex, except maybe once with his dad. And that had only been to get pregnant.

His ears perked up when he caught the end of the conversation. "What's an aptitude test?" he asked.

"It's a test I took where they ask a bunch of questions about what you like and don't like and then predict what kind of jobs you'll be good at."

"Cool. What kind of jobs did yours say?"

"It, um, said…I'm good working with my hands."

"They never saw you, huh?" Jake's tone was matter-of-fact.

"Nope."

He tilted his head. "Would you have scored twice as much if you had two hands?"

"Jake!" His mom acted shocked, as if she hadn't been thinking the same thing.

"What? I just wondered."

"That's a rude question."

"Sorry," Jake mumbled. Then he brightened. He thought Royce was about the most interesting guy in the world. "What else are you good at?"

"It says teaching, art and sales."

"Hmm. I don't see you as a salesman," his mom said.

"Yeah, I interviewed for a telemarketer job and they said the same thing, just because I didn't think I could sell magazine subscriptions to little old ladies who didn't need them."

"What about art? Painting only takes one hand," Jake pointed out. "And anyone can be a teacher."

His mom gave him The Look. "I've volunteered in the classroom and I can tell you it takes a lot more skill than you kids realize."

"I don't think I'm cut out to be a teacher,"

Royce said. "At least not with little bitty kids."

Jake patted Royce's arm. "You don't need a job. *I'm* your job."

"But we both know this is just a temporary gig, Jake. Till I find a real job and your mother finds a new nanny." He turned to Jake's mom. "Any progress with the agencies?"

"No, but I'm on the waiting list and I call every week to find out what's happening."

Jake's ice cream melted down the side of his cone and onto his hand. All of a sudden, it didn't taste good anymore. But then he got to thinking. He just had to figure out a way to make Royce stay on permanently. Or at least until Jake was thirteen and could stay home alone.

KATY OPENED THE ENVELOPE—no return address. Inside was a hundred-dollar check from Eddie.

She stared at the check long and hard, wishing it would disappear. Sure, she could use the money. But it was only a drop in the bucket compared to the total back support he owed. It bothered her all the same.

What was Eddie up to?

"I DON'T WANT to talk about it," Royce said through clenched teeth.

"I'm telling ya, buddy, she wants you. Warm for your form and all that. Time to get back in the saddle." Gus adjusted the weight machine.

"Look, when I'm ready to get back in the saddle, as you put it, I can handle it. I don't need a cheering section."

"You're passing up a prime opportunity. You should have heard her at the three-legged race—practically announced to the world that you're her man."

"I find that hard to believe." Though it did make him feel good. "Katy is a wonderful woman and any man would be lucky to have her. But I'm not going to start something I can't finish."

"Can't finish? You got problems in the lower extremities?"

"Not *that* kind of problem." Unfortunately, his libido was alive and kicking and demanding attention these days. "I don't have a clue what I'm going to do with my life. Katy deserves better than that."

"Convenient."

"It's a fact. Eight months ago, I knew what I wanted out of life. My next job was always the best employment opportunity in a place I wanted to explore."

Gus's expression was somber. "No, I meant it was a convenient excuse. You're hiding behind not knowing exactly what life is going to bring. I've got news for you. *None* of us knows for sure what's going to happen."

"It's not the same."

Gus crossed his arms over his chest. "You talk to your son lately?"

"No, just that one short phone conversation."

"Are you going to leave it at that?"

"Hell, yes. I tried. I'm not going to crowd him."

Gus shook his head. He picked up a damp towel and slung it over his shoulder. "You're a coward, Royce, pure and simple. We're done for the day."

"Tell me something I don't know," Royce muttered under his breath.

Gus really pissed him off, because the guy was single and childless and had no right to lecture Royce about his relationships.

But Royce was annoyed most by the way Gus acted as if Royce's losing his hand and livelihood shouldn't affect how he saw himself, how he compared himself to other men…how women compared him to other men.

And, truth be told, he wanted Gus to be right about that. Wanted it so badly it hurt.

# CHAPTER ELEVEN

KATY HELPED HERSELF to another slice of pepperoni pizza while listening to Jake chatter about the A he'd received on his Oregon project.

Savoring melted mozzarella and tangy sauce, she came to the conclusion that pizza was another of Royce's specialties. She suspected he was a man of many talents.

*Don't even go there.*

It was hard not to, though. Coming home at night to the aroma of a home-cooked meal and the sight of a handsome man in her kitchen was pretty seductive. Add easygoing, wide-ranging conversations and it wasn't hard to imagine taking it to a more intimate level.

Katy's face grew warm. She had nothing to be ashamed of. She was a red-blooded,

American woman who put her child first. That didn't necessarily preclude having a sex life.

Oh, who was she fooling? She'd mostly lived like a nun in order to devote herself to Jake.

Her conscience nagged. Sure, part of it was Jake. But part of it was not wanting to get burned again.

"What do you think?" Royce asked.

Katy blinked. "About what?"

"About Jake having a birthday party? His birthday is on May third, isn't it?"

"Yeah, Mom, you don't even have to get me presents or anything. Just a party."

Katy stalled for time, pretending to chew her pizza carefully. "You know I don't do birthday parties."

"That's okay. Royce can do it all. You just show up." Jake's expression was so hopeful it almost melted her heart.

But that itchy, claustrophobic feeling started, as if the room was suddenly too warm. "I don't think so, Jake, that's an awful lot to ask."

"Dad'd let me have a party."

"He would do no such thing."

"He said so."

"You've talked to your father?"

"He came by the bus stop today and we talked for a minute."

Katy thought she might be ill. But somehow she managed to keep her cool. "Why?"

"'Cause he misses me. The new baby's going to be a girl and he wants me to be her big brother. So we can be a real family."

"That's what he said?"

"Uh-huh."

She glanced at Royce, hoping he could somehow make this go away. She knew her eyes were probably as big as silver dollars.

"I'm sure it's nothing," he said, grasping her hand.

"Daddy said he'd call you, Mom."

"It would have been nice if he'd done that in the first place," she commented drily.

"Hey, buddy, why don't you take your pizza into the front room and watch a movie while I discuss the party with your mom?"

Jake nodded, his expression suddenly mature. "Sure."

When he was gone, Royce asked, "Are you okay?"

"I was afraid something like this would happen. Eddie sends me one child support payment and then thinks he can come in and pick up where he left off with Jake."

"Why don't you wait to see what he has to say? Maybe give him a call tonight?"

Katy scraped the hair back from her forehead. "This is my worst nightmare come true."

"It doesn't have to be. Give him the benefit of the doubt. Maybe he's realizing how important his relationship with his son is."

"And what if he's not? What if this is just some whim? I don't think Jake can take another disappointment."

"Jake…or you?"

His quiet question hurt more than she could have imagined. "It's not that at all."

"Okay. Just thought I'd ask. Because if Eddie is sincere, it's a good thing for Jake to have a relationship with him."

"Easy for you to say." Understanding dawned. Easy, because he could only see the estranged father's side.

And she was too afraid of losing her son to give him the benefit of the doubt.

KATY SAT DOWN with a cup of herbal tea in her hand and pulled Jake's baby album toward her on the coffee table. She never tired of thumbing through the book. In the beginning, there were tons of photos showing Eddie and his son. Later, they were all Jake. Because, of course, Katy was the photographer.

She removed her address book from her purse to find Eddie's most recent phone number. Then she picked up the phone and dialed. When a female answered, she said, "This is Katy, Jake's mom. May I speak to Eddie?"

Soon Eddie was on the line. They hadn't spoken in several months—since he'd told her to get off his back.

"I meant to call you." Was his tone defensive?

"Jake said you met him after school."

"Yeah, I, um, wanted to talk to him."

"You could have let me know."

"I wanted to spend some time just me and him, without you getting in the middle of it."

"I'm not stopping you from doing that. But it…makes me nervous when you approach him out of the blue when I'm not around."

"He's my son. I don't need your permission."

"I don't want to fight, Eddie. All I'm saying is I'd like to know next time. I don't think that's too much to ask."

"I guess not."

"Are you planning on seeing him again?"

"Yeah. Maybe have him come spend the weekend before the baby comes so we can get to know each other again."

Katy took a deep breath. "Why now?"

"I'm trying to be more of a family man. I want his baby sister to know him. Brianna does, too."

"Just…be careful."

"What do I need to be careful about?"

"Hurting Jake."

"You always think the worst of me. Of course I'm not going to hurt my own son."

*Of course not.* Just as he hadn't hurt Jake the other times he'd disappointed the boy who had ended up crying himself to sleep.

Or telling Katy he hated *her* before stomping off to his room. But she restrained herself from flinging that information back at Eddie.

"It might be a good idea to start off slow. Jake hasn't spent much time with you lately."

*You're virtually a stranger to him.*

"Yeah, so you can hover and run interference and make sure we never get a minute alone. Our custody papers say I get him every other weekend. I'll pick him up a week from Friday after school."

"Not this Friday?"

"No, I've got something going on."

Of course he did. And something would probably come up the next weekend, as it always did. But she didn't have a choice, or so her attorney had told her. Being an inconsistent dad wasn't a crime. With no indication of abuse, all he had to demonstrate was a desire to see his son.

Katy sighed. "I guess that's okay, especially since I'll be home this weekend and want to spend time with Jake. I'll be out of town next weekend subbing for a coworker, but you can pick him up at my apartment— the nanny will be here."

After she hung up, Katy realized Eddie hadn't even asked to speak to his son. She'd intentionally waited to call till Jake was asleep, but Eddie couldn't have known that.

She had a bad feeling about his sudden interest.

ROYCE READ THE LETTER one more time. His former employer had reconsidered their position regarding his injury. They would retroactively pay disability, which was reflected in the enclosed check. Enough for a down payment on a truck and a small cushion for savings. They would also reimburse certain retraining/education expenses.

Closing his eyes for a moment, Royce enjoyed the surreal moment, knowing the worst of his struggles were over. He almost expected the letter to disintegrate like those on *Mission: Impossible*.

He opened his eyes, contemplating a future that hadn't seemed feasible a couple of months ago. If he received the partial disbursement on his investments that he'd requested, he might just have room to breathe. Then he could decide what to do with the second half of his life. And ease out of the nanny gig.

*No way.*

His reaction was instant and unequivocal.

The nanny gig, unexpected and offbeat though it was, got him out of bed every day. He looked forward to his time with Jake more than he'd anticipated. And spending time with Katy was…nice.

However, he was confident Katy would find a replacement nanny in due time and by then he'd have a backup plan in place.

KATY DIDN'T STOP to ask herself why she was at Royce's door yet again. She needed to talk to someone and he had become her friend.

"Is this a bad time?" she asked when he opened the door, dressed only in a low-slung pair of shorts.

"No, it's fine. Come on in. I'll go put a shirt on."

Katy almost said, "Don't," as she entered the apartment, but managed to stop herself. Barely.

The sight of his bare back was enough to

make her raise an eyebrow. For some reason, she'd never noticed Royce was an exceptionally well-built guy. Muscular, yet lean.

He returned, pulling a T-shirt over his head. "What's up?"

"Jake's asleep. I—I didn't think it would hurt to leave him alone if I dashed right back."

"He'll be okay for a couple minutes. I stayed alone far longer when I was his age. Talk to me."

"I wanted to let you know you won't have to watch Jake next weekend when I'm out of town. I'll still pay you, though." She knew his finances were tight and didn't want to penalize him for the sudden change in plans.

"Your auction get canceled? Or is the regular auctioneer recovered enough from his surgery to make it?"

"Neither, I'm afraid. Eddie's, um, taking Jake for the weekend. He'll pick him up at my place on Friday afternoon."

Royce sat on the couch and patted the seat next to him.

She sank down, grateful to have someone with whom to share her worries.

Royce turned toward her, their knees briefly touching.

Katy shifted, uncomfortable with the way her body responded to such an innocuous touch.

Clearing his throat, Royce asked, "It's none of my business, but isn't a whole weekend kind of rushing things? It doesn't sound like Jake knows the guy all that well."

"I asked him to take it slow. But Eddie's not big on patience. And he's within his rights."

"Even if it might mess up Jake?"

She nodded. "Believe me, I don't like it, either. But there's nothing I can do unless I have tangible proof Eddie's an unfit father. And for Jake's sake, I have to hope Eddie's sincere this time."

"But?"

"But a part of me just wants to keep things the way they are. Up till now, I've been able to raise Jake as I see fit. I'm…scared Eddie's going to want to mess with that. And what if he's thinking about asking for joint custody? That would kill me."

Royce grasped her hand. "That's not going to happen."

"How do you know?"

He sighed. "I don't. All I know is that you're the best possible parent for Jake and that should be obvious to anyone who sees you."

Royce's confidence in her was unexpected and welcome. He continued to hold her hand, his reassuring warmth encouraging her to confide her biggest fear. "You don't understand. Soon, Eddie will be able to offer the one thing I can't—a two-parent home, with a sibling thrown in. Factor in the travel involved with my job and I wouldn't be surprised if a judge awarded primary custody to Eddie. What am I going to do?"

"Calm down. Nobody's going to let that happen. Why don't you just see how this weekend goes? He might not even show up. Or if he does, he might get tired of the whole daddy thing pretty quickly."

Katy held his gaze, trying to see into his mind, into his heart. His belief in her was real.

She touched his face, as if absorbing his reassurance through her fingertips. Slowly, the panicky feeling eased from her chest.

"Thank you."

He placed a kiss on her palm. "Anytime, babe, anytime."

How many times had she wished for a man to be there for her one hundred percent? Not just when it was convenient and not just when he felt like it, but consistently, without reservation. Katy felt a glimmer of hope that Royce might prove to be that kind of guy.

It was very tempting to lean close and kiss him, but totally unwise given the complicated nature of both their lives. Instead, Katy tried to rein in her emotions.

"Did Jake tell you about the school carnival Wednesday night?" she asked, changing the subject.

Royce let go of her hand. "Yeah, I think he might have said something about that. Big fund-raiser, lots of games and food. Maybe even a live band?"

"I wondered if you'd like to go with us? It's usually a lot of fun."

"Sure."

"No need to cook Wednesday night, then. I'll spring for dinner at the carnival."

"Sounds good. So I'll plan to see Jake off

to his dad's on Friday. Then Saturday and Sunday are mine?"

"Yes. I should be back before Eddie brings him home on Sunday. If he even follows through."

Katy turned away so he couldn't see the hope in her eyes. Hope that Eddie would simply disappear again for months, maybe even years. Because that would mean Jake wouldn't get attached, only to have his heart broken again.

## CHAPTER TWELVE

"ARE YOU REALLY GOING with us to the carnival tonight?" Jake asked, working on his homework at the kitchen table.

Royce said, "You bet. Can't wait."

"I, uh, forgot to tell Mom that we're supposed to bring something for the bake sale."

"I think we can crank something out before she gets home. What did you have in mind?"

"Rice Krispies Treats. Yours are the best."

Royce felt a spark of pride. There were many things he couldn't do now. But he was learning new skills, too, and dammit, he was becoming one heck of a cook.

"Thanks, kid. Let's check the kitchen for ingredients."

Jake raced ahead of Royce. He inspected the cupboards. "Cereal, but no marshmallows."

"I have some down at my place."

They retrieved the marshmallows and got to work. By the time Katy arrived home, the mixture was cut into bars and placed on plates. With two of them working, especially with Royce's increased dexterity, the job didn't take long at all.

"Ohh, Rice Krispies Treats, my favorite." She grabbed one off the plate.

"Come on, Mom, let's go. Dusty and Adam are going to be there by six. Chris is coming later."

"Let me change clothes first." She headed toward her bedroom, but stopped halfway. "Who are Dusty and Adam?"

"My new friends. We've been hanging out since Chris's birthday party. I want to invite them to my party, okay?"

"I never said you were having a party, Jake. I said I'd think about it."

"That usually means no." He raised his chin, the light of battle in his eyes.

"I don't want to discuss it anymore tonight. When I've made a decision, I'll let you know."

"But—"

"No buts, Jake. Or the answer's a definite no."

"Okay." His voice was glum.

She heard Royce murmur to him as she turned and went to her room. Quickly pulling on her favorite pair of jeans, her hand hovered over the hangers when it came time to pick a shirt. She had a couple of cute new T-shirts. And then there was the halter top she'd bought on a whim.

Shaking her head, she chose a safe hunter-green T-shirt, since dressing to seduce was not a good idea at such a family-oriented event. Especially since her life was too complicated for her to seriously consider seduction.

Katy ran a comb through her hair, freshened her makeup and was ready to go. Entering the front room, she asked, "You guys ready?"

"Sure." Royce picked up the plate of treats and Jake came trotting out from his room. "Let's go!"

His excitement was contagious and Katy felt a welcome wave of optimism. Maybe things were looking up. Maybe by this time next week all her fears about Eddie would be merely a fading blip on the radar screen.

Humming under her breath, she grasped Jake's hand.

"Mom, I don't hold hands anymore."

Slowly, she released him. "Sorry, I forgot."

"Hey, kid, why don't you carry these?" Royce gave the plate of snacks to Jake.

"Sure. Can I have one?"

"After we eat," Royce and Katy said in unison.

"Jake may not hold hands anymore, but I do. I put the kid to work so I could do this." Royce grasped her hand.

She laughed, enjoying the way her hand felt cocooned in his. "I totally approve."

Not only did she approve, but she wanted more. More touching, more closeness, more feeling as if she belonged to someone, heart and soul. But did she have the courage to pursue something like that with Royce?

Royce absorbed the warmth of Katy's smile, enjoying the flash of interest in her eyes. He liked knowing she found him attractive and he liked making her smile.

"Food first or games?" he asked.

"Definitely food. My stomach's growling. Is that okay with you, Jake?"

"Yeah. I bet my friends are at the food area already, since you took so long getting ready."

Katy rolled her eyes. "Just be glad it wasn't formal, or I could have taken *hours*."

The boy groaned. "You're kidding, right?"

"If she's a typical female, she's dead serious. You'll soon learn firsthand that there's preparation time involved for females to look and smell as good as they do."

Jake shot him a glare.

Royce laughed. "You may not believe me now. I'll check back with you in a couple years."

"There's Dusty. Can I go, Mom?"

"As long as you stick with Dusty and check back every half hour."

"Sure." Jake ran off without a backward look.

Katy nudged Royce with her shoulder. "Is that what I have to look forward to for the next eight years? Seeing the back of him as he charges off to find another adventure?"

"Yep, pretty much. Only soon, he'll be off in search of those sweet-smelling girls."

"He's only ten."

Royce squeezed her hand. "I know. They grow up quick."

She frowned and he tried to think of something to distract her. He veered down another aisle with booths on either side.

"My stomach tells me the food is this way."

Smiling, she said, "My nose agrees. The flyer said we'd have our choice of hot dogs, hamburgers and Mexican food, catered, of course, with a portion of the proceeds benefitting the school."

"In that case, I'm definitely hungry."

"Let me stop at the ticket booth. Remember, this is my treat."

That didn't sit well with Royce. He'd always paid his own way. And for some reason, it was doubly important Katy didn't think he was a mooch.

"I can get it."

"No, I invited you. It's only fair, since you cook dinner most nights."

"That's part of my job. This is different."

Tilting her head to the side, she said,

"Please? It's important to me. You can pay next time."

"How can I say no?"

She grinned. "I was hoping you couldn't."

He tried to assuage his wounded pride by admiring the view as she stepped up to the ticket booth. Even in jeans, he could tell her legs were long and lean and the rest of her was shaped nicely, too.

"Hey, Royce, where's my mom?" Jake was breathless, his cheeks red, as if he'd been running.

Royce corralled his thoughts and nodded toward the booth. "Getting tickets." He nodded at Jake's friend. "Hi, Dusty."

"Hi. Can Jake come eat with me and my family? They're over there." He pointed toward a picnic table where a family was already eating.

"Why don't you ask your mom, Jake?"

Katy walked toward them as he asked permission.

She nodded, handing Jake a bunch of tickets. "I didn't realize it, but I've met Dusty's mom before on field trips. Just be sure to check in like I asked."

Royce and Katy waved at Dusty's parents and went to get their own food. When they received their plates, Katy's was piled high with beans, rice and a burrito. "Good thing I'm hungry."

Royce braced a can of pop against his chest with his forearm while he grasped his plate with his right hand. He ignored the few folks who stared. He knew they'd glance away if he met their gazes.

"If not, I'm sure Jake can finish it off for you. That boy can eat."

"I don't know where he puts it all," she said. "How about over there?" She nodded toward one small table among the other industrial-size picnic tables.

What could have been an awkward moment became a nonissue. Katy didn't seem to mind that people stared. Or that some tasks took longer for him.

"Great."

They sat down and made small talk and ate. A few moments later, Jake ran up.

"Is it okay if I go play games now?"

"Sure."

"Oh, and Mom?"

"Yes?"

"I'm gonna have a birthday party, aren't I? The guys want to know."

Katy's voice was strained when she said, "I told you I'd think about it. Now, scoot."

Royce leaned close and lowered his voice. "D'you want to talk about it?"

"No."

"Not here or not ever?"

She sipped her drink, avoiding his gaze. He wondered if she would avoid his question, too.

Finally, she said, "Maybe we can talk some other time."

He squeezed her hand. "Anytime. I mean it."

And he did. She'd seen past his injury and treated him as a man. He intended to see past whatever her issue was and support her, as well. Because he had no doubt there was a wound she was hiding.

Royce was honored that she trusted him enough to at least consider sharing her secrets.

ROYCE ANSWERED THE DOOR Friday afternoon and couldn't have been more shocked if Eddie had been a flesh-eating zombie. The guy was medium height, a little on the scrawny side, with stringy brown hair. His close-set eyes narrowed as he looked Royce up and down.

"I must have the wrong apartment."

"You're Eddie?" Royce asked, blocking the doorway with his body. He wasn't too sure he wanted this guy near Jake. And he didn't even want to think about Katy having been married to the man.

"Yeah. This is Katy Garner's place, right? I'm here for Jake."

Royce hesitated. "Come in. Jake's waiting." As a matter of fact the kid was so excited, Royce wouldn't have been surprised if Jake had bowled him over to get to his father.

But the boy hung back, his shoulders hunched.

"Jake, your dad's here." Royce kept his voice low and reassuring.

"Hi, Dad."

"Hey, Jakie. Come give me a hug."

Jake allowed himself to be hugged, but his arms remained at his sides.

"We're gonna have a good time this weekend. We've rented a four-bedroom house, so you'll have your own room. Then there's a nursery for the baby."

"Cool." There was a spark of interest in Jake's eyes.

Royce wished Katy was there. Should he encourage Jake to go with a man who was a virtual stranger? He didn't want to allow the guy out of his sight. But what choice did he have?

Now he understood why Katy had been so nervous about Eddie. The man didn't inspire confidence. But Royce reminded himself that Eddie was trying to rebuild a relationship with his son. That should count for something. And who was he to judge another man for being a bad father? He was living proof it was never too late to change.

"So do you live here?" Eddie asked, challenge tingeing his voice.

"No, I'm a neighbor."

"Katy said the nanny would be here."

"I *am* the nanny." Some primal instinct made Royce step forward and get in the guy's face.

"Oh, um, sure man." Eddie glanced down at Royce's left arm. His eyes widened. "Katy always did like to collect strays."

Rage built inside Royce. He clenched his fist, experiencing power in the knowledge he could lay this weasel out with one punch. Missing hand or not.

Apparently Eddie came to the same conclusion. "Come on, Jake, let's go. Brianna's waiting in the car."

"You left your pregnant, um, wife, waiting in a hot car?"

"She's got the keys. She can run the air-conditioning."

Royce almost called Jake back as he trudged toward the door with Eddie, his backpack slung over his shoulder.

Instead, he cleared his throat and said, "Be good, Jake," when he really meant, "Stay safe."

Jake hesitated. He ran back to Royce and hugged him quickly. Then turned and was gone.

Royce closed the door slowly. He went to Jake's room and sank down on the bed, feeling as if he'd just made a huge mistake.

Squeezing his eyes shut, he ignored the hot tears trickling down his face.

This felt like hell. He didn't know how Katy could stand it.

# CHAPTER THIRTEEN

ON SUNDAY, KATY UNLOCKED the door and stood in the entryway to her empty apartment. There was no food cooking, no reassuring banter between Jake and Royce.

Katy felt as if a part of her had died.

*Jake will be back in a few hours.*

Still, she had to concentrate hard on breathing. Panic was waiting, ready to pounce if she let it.

Katy forced herself to focus on routine tasks, taking her suitcase to her bedroom, putting away her toiletries. She glanced in Jake's room, but didn't go in. It wouldn't help matters if Eddie brought him back and she was curled up in the fetal position on the bed.

Katy went to the kitchen and microwaved hot water for a cup of tea. On the counter, she found a plate of Royce's signature treats. Attached was a note. "Thought you might need these—R."

Wiping her eyes, she sat down at the breakfast bar with her cup of herbal tea and a large, chewy square. She was truly fortunate to have found a friend like Royce.

A few minutes later, there was a knock at her door.

Katy jumped up, but forced herself to walk instead of run.

She took a deep breath, pasted on a bright smile and opened the door. Her shoulders sagged. "Oh, it's you. Come on in, Royce."

"I'd be offended by your greeting, but I know you have to be on pins and needles."

"I'm sorry. I thought you were Jake."

"I know, sweetheart." He opened his arms to her and she gladly accepted refuge there. Though she tried to retain control, she started to sob.

Royce smoothed her hair, murmuring reassurances.

With her face resting against his chest, she poured out her doubts and worries. All the crazy scenarios that had run through her mind over the weekend. How she kept expecting to get a call that Jake was scared or lost or hurt.

Royce rubbed her shoulder while she cried.

When the tears stopped, Katy leaned back. "I'm sorry. I'm sure this wasn't what you bargained for when you came up here."

"This is *exactly* what I bargained for. I figured you might need me."

"I'm usually not weepy like this."

"And you usually don't have to allow your son to go with someone you're not sure is trustworthy."

"Yes." She stepped out of his arms, embarrassed about the way she'd blubbered all over him. "Thank you for understanding."

"Maybe I understand better than you know."

"How's that? Something to do with Michael?"

He shook his head. "Maybe I'll tell you sometime."

At another time, her curiosity might have been piqued, but not today.

Glancing at her watch, she sighed. Only

three o'clock. "Jake shouldn't be back for another two hours. Still, I guess I'd hoped he might be home early."

"The place is pretty quiet without him, huh?"

"Totally."

"You want me to leave, so you can go soak in a bath or whatever women do to unwind?"

Katy shook her head. "The bath sounds great, but I'm too stressed if that makes sense. I kind of need to use the nervousness to keep going. Would you mind staying and just talking for a while?"

"Not at all."

She heard his stomach growl. "Some really nice guy left a plate of goodies. Any chance I can convince you to try one?"

"Twist my arm."

"Tea? Coffee?"

"Water's good."

She went to the kitchen, retrieved the plate and placed it on the coffee table. Grabbing a water bottle from the fridge, she handed it to him.

"Thanks." He sat on the couch and took the cap off the bottle.

"How was your auction?"

"Good. Except I was pretty distracted. I kept hoping the headhunter didn't have someone in the audience checking me out. I get nervous when I think that his client might be one of the top houses like Sinclair or Barrett-Jackson."

"You never know. But I bet you work well under pressure. And I know you have the ability to think on your feet, raising a kid as smart as Jake."

"I have my moments. A mentor would be nice, but most of the guys are pretty intent on protecting their turf. Herb will be eager to take back his slot, and other women are still few and far between."

"You can do it with or without a mentor. You've got what it takes."

Katy held his statement close to her heart. She so rarely heard praise these days. Her boss generally took her for granted and her mother was, well, her mother. Clearing her throat, she said, "That means a lot coming from you, Royce."

He glanced around the room, as if she'd revealed too much.

Katy searched for a safer topic. "How's your job hunting going?"

"Not even a nibble. I have to admit I haven't been hitting it very hard."

"Oh?"

He leaned forward. "I'm trying to come up with a plan. Figure out what I really want to do with my life instead of jumping into something, anything, just to get moving."

"I can understand that. Sometimes I feel like I'm in a rut."

"You've got a son to raise. That's the most important job in the world. There will be plenty of time for other things."

"I bet you didn't feel that way when Michael was growing up."

"No. But I'd sure do things differently if I could."

"Do you have any idea what you want to do?"

Royce took another drink, as if stalling for time. "I love welding and I'm good at it. Was good at it, that is. I'd thought about maybe teaching at a tech school or high school, but let's face it, I can't teach proper technique with one hand."

Hesitating, she asked, "How about a prosthesis?"

"I tried one out early on and it irritated my skin. Didn't really give me enough dexterity, either. I may give it another try later on, but I'll never have the coordination that I once did."

"So working in the mines is definitely out of the question? There's nothing related you could do?"

"Just administration and I wouldn't be happy tied to a desk all day." He bit into his square. After he'd chewed and swallowed, he commented, "It's funny. I expected to be impatient to get out of the country again, but things are…different now."

"Michael?"

"Yeah, that's part of it. I guess I'm starting to feel like I've been given a second chance at life."

Katy wondered if the accident was solely responsible for his change in attitude or if she and Jake had anything to do with it. "You've kind of…taken to the nanny thing better than I expected."

He held up his hand. "Not nanny."

"I mean, Kid Wrangler."

"That's better. Jake's made it easy. He's a great kid."

"And maybe you're at a point in your life where you're better at being around kids?"

"Old and boring?"

Katy smiled. She couldn't imagine him ever seeming old. He was too vital, too intense. "Not hardly."

He took a swig of water. "I don't know, I guess with Jake I feel like I'm contributing something."

"Wasn't that how you felt with Michael?"

"No. I didn't want Tess to leave him alone with me. I was afraid I'd screw it up. And she had very definite ideas on Michael's care. So it was easier just to let her do it all."

"Easier than risking failure, I bet. Kind of scary to let down a child when he's depending on you."

"Absolutely. But it was worse than just letting Michael down. I was afraid I might put him in jeopardy."

Katy opened her mouth to respond, but clamped it shut.

"What?"

"Nothing."

"It's something. What were you going to say?"

"I was going to say that maybe you took the easy way out, but seeing how badly it tears you up, I don't think that was the case."

"For a minute there I thought you might have me confused with Eddie."

"There are...some similarities."

Disappointment flashed in his eyes. "That's too bad."

Katy reached for his hand. "I'm sorry. I know you're not like Eddie. Sometimes it's hard not to get my stuff all mixed up with yours."

"Eddie's a crummy dad, I was a crummy dad."

Katy gazed up at him, willing him to understand. "I respect you, Royce, you've been a good friend to me and to Jake. I'm in no position to judge."

"Yet you do." Royce's quiet words cut deep.

He looked so sad, she wanted to make things better. Angling her head, she kissed him, gently, persistently, to show him how sorry she was to have hurt him. And to let him know how much he'd come to mean to her. But mostly, it was simply because it felt right.

His shoulders stiffened and she feared that he might pull away. But with a sigh, he returned her kiss, nudging her lips apart and exploring her.

He was giving her a second chance and for that she was grateful. Twining her arms around his neck, she drew him close, murmuring his name. Inhaling his taste and scent and sinking into something with no beginning, no ending.

Groaning, Royce held her snugly to him. He slipped his hand beneath her shirt, sliding his fingers up her rib cage. She sucked in a breath. It had been so long since a man had touched her like this.

Friendship, discovery, awe, all were a part of the experience as he deepened the kiss. For once, Katy felt free to let go. Grasping his hand, she placed it on her breast.

He felt for her bra clasp. She could tell he smiled when he found it was in front. With a flick of the wrist, he freed her breasts and ran his palm over the swell. His fingers teased while he kissed her again, deeply, thoroughly.

Katy traced the line of his shoulders, the planes of his chest, wanting nothing more than to rid him of the clothing that got in her way. Leaning back, she drew him with her.

His weight was welcome on top of her. She shifted, trying to get closer to him.

She opened her eyes in surprise as he ended the kiss. "What?"

He traced the curve of her cheek with his fingers, brushing them against her mouth. "Are you sure you want this?"

"Absolutely."

The doorbell rang. She briefly rested her forehead against Royce's. "Bad timing?"

"Horrible."

The doorbell rang again and Katy scrambled to her feet, closing her bra as she went. She straightened her shirt and ran a hand through her hair.

Katy was reaching for the knob as she heard a key turn in the lock. The horror of what might have happened registered. She'd very nearly been busted by...

"Jake, Eddie."

Jake ran inside and gave her a big hug. "Hi, Mom."

"Come in," she said to Eddie.

"I can't stay." But he came inside, anyway.

"Did you have a good time, honey?"

"Yeah, I've got my own room at Dad's house and everything. A Wii set, too. Can you believe it?"

"No, I mean, yes. That's wonderful." Katy supposed to a ten-year-old boy it *was* wonderful. To her, it looked like smoke and mirrors.

"Royce, you'd really like the video games I got at Dad's."

Eddie's gaze settled on Royce. "What's the nanny doing here when there's no kid?"

Katy raised her chin. "I don't have to explain myself to you. Don't let me keep you." She headed for the door.

"I get the picture. I'm not sure I want my son exposed to this kind of stuff."

Strangling a cry of disbelief, Katy asked, "And what about you and your pregnant girlfriend?"

"We went to Vegas a couple weeks ago.

Brianna's my wife now. Looks like I'm the responsible one these days, doesn't it? I'll expect to pick up Jake next Friday, same time."

"You're only supposed to get him every other weekend."

"I've got a lot of lost time to make up for. I'm sure you won't try to keep me from my son." He opened the door and left.

## CHAPTER FOURTEEN

ROYCE SAW FEAR FLASH in Katy's eyes and knew without a doubt that she'd received Eddie's threat loud and clear.

He could have gladly punched the guy.

The irony made him sad. Who knew what stupid stuff Royce might have said in a similar situation? But that was then, this was now.

He hesitated, touching Katy's shoulder. "I better go, unless you need me…to stay." Holding his breath, he hoped she did need him. They were leaving an awful lot up in the air.

Her smile wobbled a bit. "I'll be fine. We'll talk later."

Releasing his breath, he ruffled Jake's hair. "You have a good day at school tomorrow, okay?"

"Sure." Jake barely glanced up from his handheld video game.

Royce felt like hired help, but knew he had only himself to blame. He could have been honest with Katy. Let her know that he understood how upset she was and that he needed to be there for her. Partly because of the shift in their relationship and partly because she was, first and foremost, his friend.

But with Eddie's attitude, it probably would have only added fuel to the fire.

Royce went to his apartment and listened to the footsteps upstairs. He hadn't been this lonely since waking up in a German hospital, unable to recognize his own son.

JAKE GLANCED SIDEWAYS at Royce as they walked to the park. Royce had been pretty quiet.

"It's really cool we can go play catch today. Thanks."

"Sure, kid, no problem."

Jake tossed the baseball up into the air and caught it in his mitt without missing a step. He thought he was getting pretty good.

"I got picked fourth today."

"For what?"

"Baseball. The kids have noticed I got a lot better. They don't say I throw like a girl anymore."

"That's really great, Jake." Royce smiled, almost like his old self.

"Are you mad at my mom?"

"No, why'd you think that?"

"'Cause you left so fast Sunday. And my mom seemed sad."

"Maybe she's got something on her mind."

"Like my dad?"

"What do you think?"

"I think maybe she's worried I'll start loving my dad more than her."

"You may be right. It's just been your mom and you for a long time."

"Uh-huh." For as long as Jake could remember. Other than their rare outings, he had only vague memories of his dad living with them, and they could have been dreams.

Royce patted Jake's shoulder. "It'll probably just take some time for her to adjust to sharing you."

Since Royce was back to acting like

himself, Jake figured he could ask him something else that had been bothering him. "How come my dad doesn't like my mom?"

"Well…I can't say about your mom and dad. But when my wife and I divorced, both of us had hurt feelings. So sometimes we acted mad instead of letting our pain show."

Jake thought about it for a minute. That made sense. He tried really hard not to let the kids at school know when they hurt his feelings. Sometimes he'd rather say something mean than have them think he was a wimp.

Then an awful thought surfaced. "Did I make them mad?"

"No, absolutely not. It's grown-up stuff, Jake, it had nothing to do with you. They both love you in their own ways."

"I feel kind of weird at my dad's house. Like I don't belong…and I miss my mom."

Royce knelt down next to him. "It's natural to miss your mom, kid. My mom died a long time ago and I *still* miss her."

"You do?" Jake had a hard time believing that. Royce was so big and strong and good at everything. But he'd never lied to Jake.

"I sure do. You'll get used to your dad's

house, too. I figure it's kind of like the start of the school year. You know, the first time you walk into your new classroom?"

"Yeah?"

"Everything seems strange. The desks are in different places, there are different kids in your class, a new teacher."

Jake nodded.

"After two weeks, it seems like you've been there forever."

Relief washed over Jake. "Yeah, like it's always been that way."

"Absolutely. I bet your father's house will seem like that soon, too."

"I just gotta be patient?"

"Exactly."

They walked in silence for a few minutes. Then Jake remembered something else confusing.

"Royce, how come my dad doesn't like you?"

He glanced up to see surprise flicker over Royce's face.

Then Royce adjusted his baseball cap, as if the sun had gotten in his eyes. "I don't know, kid. I don't know."

ROYCE WITHDREW THE CHECK from the envelope. One of his investments had finally come through—enough for a down payment on a car. Excitement coursed through him. After relying on the Phoenix bus system, he felt like a sixteen-year-old anticipating his first car.

Flipping open his wallet, he removed the card Gus had given him—for a guy who would sell him a reliable vehicle and modify it to make steering easier.

He whistled a tune as he sauntered out the door.

KATY WAS IN HER ROBE when there was a knock at the door on Saturday morning. Why get dressed when she was hanging around the apartment by herself all weekend?

She found Royce standing at the door, grinning. They'd somehow managed to avoid being alone together all week and here he was.

"Hi. What's up?"

"I thought maybe you might be at loose ends. Wanna go see a Cactus League baseball game? Oakland does their spring training at Phoenix Municipal Stadium."

Shrugging, Katy said, "Sure, it's better than sitting here feeling sorry for myself."

"Man, you're hard on a guy's ego. A little enthusiasm would be okay."

Her face grew warm. "I'm sorry. I didn't mean it that way. Is this, um, as friends?"

"It's anything you want it to be."

"That certainly leaves a lot of room for interpretation, especially after what happened last Sunday. Are we going to talk about it?"

"It depends. Do you want to go as friends? Or…a date?"

Katy shifted under his steady gaze. "How about if we play it by ear?"

Nodding, he said, "Then we don't need to talk about that yet, do we?"

"I guess not."

His relief was palpable. In some ways he was so different from most guys. In others, not so different. The thought made her smile.

"We need to leave if we're gonna get seats. They really bring in a crowd on the week-ends," he said.

"Come in while I get dressed." She headed for her bedroom. "Make yourself at home."

"Okay."

She threw on a T-shirt and denim shorts, dabbed on a bit of blush, mascara and lip gloss and grabbed her Diamondbacks cap.

Pulling her hair back into an elastic band, she returned to the front room. "Some advance notice would have been nice. Particularly if this is a date."

"We're just playing it by ear, remember? Works well with spontaneity."

Katy laughed. "I'm a single mom. I haven't done anything spontaneous in years."

"Then it's about time, huh?"

"I guess. It seems awfully weird without Jake, though. He would have loved the exhibition game."

"Next time we'll be sure to take him."

"Then it definitely wouldn't be a date."

"Says who?"

"Any of a number of women's magazines who recommend leaving children out of the dating scenario."

"Under normal circumstances, possibly,

but as your official Kid Wrangler, I'm a whole 'nother case entirely."

Katy tilted her head to the side. "You sure are."

"You mean that in a nice way, don't you?"

"Of course." She widened her eyes innocently. "Let's go. Do I need anything besides my keys and purse?"

"Sunscreen?"

"In my purse. I'm a redhead, it's a requirement."

His gaze lingered on the exposed flesh at her throat and chest. Need flashed in his eyes and she could tell he was recalling their kisses and caresses.

"Good. We wouldn't want you getting... burned."

Her face warmed under his concentrated gaze. Worse, her pulse accelerated, as if anticipating a repeat performance. Only this time, Jake wouldn't arrive home in time to interrupt.

The thought of Jake brought her back to reality. "Then we'll have to be very careful, won't we?" Katy playfully punched his biceps and headed toward the door, glancing at him over her shoulder.

He was laughing as he followed her out the door.

They kept up the good-natured banter as they rode the elevator down to the first level. Katy headed toward her Hyundai, but stopped when she realized Royce wasn't following her.

"My car's over here, Royce."

"Did I forget to tell you? I'm driving."

His words were so casual they almost didn't register. "*You're* driving? How?"

"Pretty much like everyone else. My SUV's over here." His smile was wide.

"When did this happen?"

"I bought it day before yesterday. They did some modifications to the steering wheel and I picked it up yesterday."

He opened the passenger door to a small SUV. "Your carriage awaits."

She settled into the front seat, slightly bemused.

Royce got in and started the engine. He expertly backed out of the space, using one hand.

"Pretty neat trick."

"I did that even when I had two hands."

"Show-off."

"Yep. But the steering wheel has been modified to make things easier."

"Wow." She couldn't keep the admiration out of her voice. "Royce, you've really bounced back from an injury that might have destroyed a lesser man."

"I've just done the best I could. I take it day by day."

"Then keep doing what you're doing."

They chatted about Jake and his school projects on their way to the ballpark.

Once there, Royce parked the SUV and pocketed the keys. "This way." He took her arm, his hand sliding down to grasp hers.

She twined her fingers in his and raised her face to the warm spring sunshine. Today was turning out to be much better than she'd expected.

## CHAPTER FIFTEEN

ROYCE WATCHED Katy cheer. Her cheeks were flushed, her eyes sparkled. He'd never seen her this animated and she was…phenomenal. He wondered if this was how she looked when she was calling auctions.

She glanced over and caught him looking.

"What? Do I have mustard on my face?" She wiped her mouth with her napkin.

"Nah, I was just watching you. I never realized you were such a fan."

"I'm not obsessed with it. But I'll watch it on TV every once in a while." She sat down next to him. "Seeing it like this is much more fun. I'll have to remember to bring Jake one of these days."

"Maybe it's more fun because of the company?"

"Are you fishing for a compliment?"

"No. Just trying to make sure you don't overlook the obvious. And we can bring Jake together, remember?"

She sighed. "I don't know about all this, Royce. I never anticipated, well…"

"Dating the nanny? If that's the case then we won't consider this a date. Problem solved."

"I haven't considered dating anyone for such a long time, at least not beyond the casual."

Royce focused on what Katy *didn't* say. That if they got involved, it would be far from casual. Was that what he wanted? He wasn't sure and he knew that wasn't fair to her.

Still, he couldn't help but ask, "Surely you've had relationships since Eddie?"

"I tried when Jake was little and it didn't work." She shrugged. "He's my world and that's the way it needs to stay. Besides, I like being friends with you. If we start…you know…getting involved, it might ruin our friendship."

"You could be right. Or it could lead to something even better."

*Damn, why had he said that?*

Katy caught his gaze. "If you're talking about what happened the other night, I don't think it's a good idea for us to repeat it."

"Because of Jake or because you're afraid? Fear I can understand. My life's been turned upside down, I'm not the same guy I used to be." His gaze strayed to his left wrist.

"With Eddie back, I don't want to rock the boat. Jake's got enough change to handle as it is."

Royce might have accused her of hiding behind her situation, except that she had a point. He'd almost forgotten about Jake. One more reason he needed to tread carefully. The last thing he wanted to do was confuse the kid or make his life harder.

Bumping her with his shoulder, he said, "I guess friendship is good, then."

Katy smiled and leaned into him. "Friendship is very good."

Royce would try to remind his libido of that. As it was, he wrapped his arm around her and tried to think of her as a buddy. But he still wanted to hold her close and never let go. Be there for her in every way a man could be there for a woman.

Ways that went beyond friendship.

The day continued with friendly cama-raderie and Royce barely considered kissing Katy when he dropped her off at her door.

*Yeah, right.*

ROYCE FORCED HIMSELF to give Katy some space, or maybe the space was for himself. Because he didn't like the fact he seemed to want more from her—stability, friendship and intimacy at levels he'd never experienced.

That thought brought his head up. He'd let down his guard with her because of Jake and now he wanted more than she was willing to give. The situation had always been reversed in the past.

All the more reason to steer clear of anything more than friendship. His resolve lasted until about noon on Sunday, when he headed for the door, intent on hashing things out with her.

The phone rang, interrupting his thoughts. He grabbed the handset on the first ring, hoping it was her.

"Hi, Royce." It was a her, but not *the* her.

"Hey, Becca. What's up?"

"The usual. Fighting kids, fighting in-laws, a cranky boss…"

"And the husband?"

She laughed. "Somehow maintaining his sanity amid the chaos and reminding me why I love him so much."

"Better hang on to that guy."

"I intend to. What's new with you? I tried calling a couple of times, but always got your voice mail."

"I've, um, got a temporary job."

"That's great. Doing what?"

"My official title is Kid Wrangler."

"Say what?"

"Kid Wrangler. It sounds more manly than nanny."

"You? A nanny? You've got to be kidding."

Her laughter wounded him. "I can be as good a nanny as the next guy."

"I'm sure you can, Royce, I just never got the impression you were all that into kids. I mean, you were great with Michael once he got older. When you were in town, that is."

"Yeah, yeah, I get the picture. You know I'm trying to make things right with him."

"Yes, I do." Her tone softened. "And I'm glad to see it."

"Hey, I didn't tell you, but I've got wheels now."

"A truck? That's great. How are you at driving it?"

"Damn good, if I do say so myself. And it's an SUV."

"My brother, the confirmed truck man driving an SUV? Next you'll tell me you want a minivan."

"I'm in the city—an SUV is more practical. Especially with the kid-wrangling gig."

"Ahh, now I think I see. Does this kid have a good-looking single mom, by any chance?"

"Katy's single." He shifted uncomfortably. "And pretty and smart and has a great heart, but what's that got to do with it?"

"Big brother, you've got it bad. I never thought I'd live to see this day. Well, at least not after things went south with you and Tess."

Royce had absolutely no intention of

letting his sister suspect that he really cared for Katy. "She's attractive and fun, okay? A lot of women are."

"But how many of them have inspired you to buy a family vehicle? Because that's what an SUV is, Royce. It's a statement to the whole world that you are finally, after all these years, ready to settle down." She chortled with glee.

"Look, Becca, I gotta go."

"Sure. Better go wax the family vehicle. I want to meet this Katy and shake her hand. She must be one terrific woman to tame the great Royce McIntyre, bachelor extraordinaire."

"Someone's at the door. Gotta go. Bye." He pressed the Off button on his phone, only slightly perturbed at lying to her.

Only it wasn't a lie, he realized. Someone *was* knocking.

He opened the door.

"Katy."

"Are you free for lunch?"

There were several off-color remarks he could have made, but he decided against alluding to all the things he was willing to give her for free.

Still, Royce couldn't help but grin when he noticed the picnic basket she carried. Whether she knew it or not, Katy was wavering in her just-friends stance.

Friends went to Starbucks or met for a burger.

Lovers had picnics.

Things were definitely looking up.

KATY TRIED TO CONCENTRATE on the road, wishing Royce didn't look as if he knew a terrific secret and had no intention of letting her in on the details.

"Aren't you the least bit curious where I'm taking you for our picnic?" she asked.

"No, I'm sure it'll be great."

She took the freeway, then surface streets to Galvin Parkway. "We're almost there."

"We're going to Papago Park? There used to be some secluded spots back in the day. Romantic at night, if I remember correctly. We used to climb to Hole-in-the-Rock."

"That's not where we're headed, but there might be some romance where I'm taking you." Katy couldn't help teasing him a bit.

"Romance is…good."

Now she felt guilty about misleading him. "Since you took me to the ball game, I wanted to do something nice in return. I shouldn't have joked about romance. Please don't misconstrue…"

"No romance, I got it."

For some reason, she still didn't think he believed her.

Turning into the parking lot for the zoo, she searched the packed aisles for a parking space.

"The zoo?"

"Yes. There's usually romance in at least one of the animal enclosures. Or so it seems, every time I bring Jake. I have to redirect his attention."

"Um, yeah."

"My mom gets us season passes. It's a nice place to picnic and maybe see some of the new babies."

"Four-legged, I hope?"

"Yes. I'm pretty sure Jake's going to be my only baby."

Royce brushed a strand of hair from her cheek. "You're a terrific mom. You should have had a whole houseful of kids."

Katy glanced down at her hands. "I don't know about a whole houseful, but two might have been nice. Only it wasn't in the cards."

"I'm sorry. I didn't mean to hit a sore spot."

She raised her face, searching his eyes and finding concern and a regret nearly as deep as her own.

He leaned forward and kissed her on the forehead. "I'm sorry," he repeated, his voice husky.

Katy resisted the urge to crawl into his lap and lose herself in his compassion.

She ran her fingertips along his face. "You're an exceptional man, Royce. And I'm glad you're my friend."

## CHAPTER SIXTEEN

ROYCE RECLINED on the picnic blanket, content in a way he hadn't anticipated. Being with Katy had that effect on him.

"You want to go see some of the exhibits?" she asked.

"Sure." He helped gather up the remains of their meal and throw it in the nearby trash can. "Where to?"

"There's a new baby giraffe I'd like to see…."

"Lead the way." Royce placed his hand at the small of her back, allowing it to linger there, enjoying the heat of her body radiating through the soft fabric.

They walked down the path, bumping together as the lane grew congested with families taking advantage of the gorgeous day.

"Did I tell you I'm interviewing with the Sinclair Auction House next week? The headhunter sent them the tape of that charity auction last month and they seem to think I should be able to move up to auctioneer with the right grooming."

"That's one of your dream houses, isn't it?"

"Yes. I'm excited…and nervous."

"You're a professional. You'll do great."

"Thanks."

They walked along in silence. Katy seemed lost in thought.

Sighing, she said, "I can't help but think the timing is horrible. What with Eddie back. If I get this job, it would mean more travel, a schedule consistently like the one I've worked while Herb's been on medical leave. That would give Eddie ammunition if he decides to fight for sole custody."

"I can't imagine a judge awarding him full custody." He shifted the picnic basket. "But you might be right about the travel in general. Jake's only going to be young once."

Katy glanced away. "Believe me, I think

about that a lot. And I wonder if this is my one shot. What if it is and I pass it up?"

"I can only tell you I've found nothing is worth risking the relationship with your child."

"Jake is the most important thing in my life. But some people seem to have it all and do fine. Why can't I be one of those people?"

The pain and confusion in her voice made him want to make it all better for her. But he couldn't.

"Maybe you can."

"You don't sound convinced."

He hesitated. "Probably because I'm not."

"The giraffe enclosure is over there." She pointed to the right and they followed the path.

Royce was only partially aware of the giraffe and her baby. Instead, he studied Katy as she watched the mother and child through the fencing, her gaze hungry, as if seeking answers from the animal world.

"You'll know when it's right to spend more time away from Jake. Just like that mama giraffe knows when her baby is mature enough to wander farther afield."

Katy was quiet. Then she glanced up at him and held his gaze. "I hope you're right."

He wrapped his arm around her shoulders and drew her close, kissing the top of her head.

*I hope so, too.*

And though the gesture might have been more than merely friendly, she seemed to accept the comfort he offered.

Her voice was muffled when she said, "I'm still going to the interview."

"I know." Royce wished he could cheer her on with his whole heart. But he suspected she was making a mistake.

KATY GROANED when they pulled into the parking lot. The day that had started out as such fun had grown more complex by the minute. "That's Eddie's car. I wonder how long he's been here?"

"He's not supposed to drop Jake off until five, right?" Royce checked his watch. "And it's only a little past three."

"I should've been here." She grabbed her purse and the picnic basket, hurrying across the parking lot.

Royce matched her stride for stride.

Anxiety made her want to break into a dead run. But she forced herself to walk.

At the elevators, Royce said, "I'll take the stairs to my floor. I had a great time. See you later."

Then he was gone.

Katy was grateful he understood. The elevator ride seemed to last forever. When she reached her apartment, she took a deep breath and unlocked the door.

Jake was playing video games and Eddie paced.

"Mom!" Jake put down his game and ran over to give her a hug.

"It's about time. We've been waiting for almost half an hour," Eddie commented.

"Hi, honey." Katy wrapped her arms around Jake. "You weren't supposed to be here until five."

"Hey, I've got things to do, too." Eddie nodded toward the picnic basket. "So where's lover boy? Oh, yeah, I forgot, you're calling him your nanny."

Katy bit back a scathing retort. "My social life is none of your business, Eddie."

"Well, it might be if I think you're not pro-viding a suitable environment for our son."

"I do just fine for Jake."

"Is that what you call—"

"Stop it." Jake pushed himself between them. "Both of you, stop fighting."

Katy's heart ached at the desperation in her son's voice. He didn't deserve to witness his pettiness. She took a deep breath. "I'm sorry, honey. It has nothing to do with you."

She rummaged in her purse until she found her business cards. Then she handed one to Eddie. "My cell number is listed on there. If you need to bring Jake home early, please call me and I'll make every effort to be here."

Eddie ran a hand through his hair. "That sounds fair. I'm, um, sorry about what I said before. Old habits die hard."

She nodded stiffly.

He said, "I'll pick him up next Friday."

"But that's his birthday," she protested. Did she dare make a big deal about this?

"I have just as much right to spend his birthday with him as you do."

Katy could see the conversation escalating toward nastiness again. She made a split-second decision. "I'm having a birthday party for him on Saturday. Why don't you and your, um, wife come? Brianna, isn't it?"

He nodded, eyeing her suspiciously. " thought you didn't like birthday parties."

That was the understatement of the year.

"I don't. But I'm willing to do this…fo Jake." She glanced at her son, his eyes wer lit with excitement. The sight almost mad her forget the knot tightening her stomach.

"Really, Mom? A party?"

"Yes, really."

He whooped for joy. "I gotta tell Royce. bet he'll help ya plan it."

Eddie stiffened at the mention of Royce but didn't say anything.

"Why don't you and Brianna come b about two o'clock?"

"Okay. We'll take Jake home with us af terward to spend the night."

"Fine." It was a reasonable solution. No great, but reasonable.

Katy sighed with relief when Eddie left.

ROYCE SET THE TABLE, letting Jake's chatte wash over him. It was a soothing jumble o ideas about birthday party themes and didn't require any answers from him.

He wondered what had prompted Katy to change her position on parties. He suspected it might have something to do with Eddie. By the time he heard Katy's key in the lock, his curiosity was simmering.

When she walked into the front room, he noticed how tired she looked. There were dark circles under her eyes and her skin was pale.

"Hey, how was your day?" he asked.

"Okay."

"Hi, Mom. Me and Royce have been thinking of party ideas. First I thought maybe we could…"

Royce tuned out the rest, concentrating instead on Katy's reaction. Her gaze darted from Jake to him to the door, as if she wanted to escape.

Royce decided he could do one of two things. Sit back and watch Katy implode. Or get active so she wouldn't have to deal with the details. His decision was simple.

"I'm pretty sure planning birthday parties falls under my job description. Do you mind if I run with it?"

Katy's look of gratitude went straight to his heart. In that moment, Royce realized he'd do just about anything for her.

She mouthed, "Thank you," over Jake's head, her eyes suspiciously bright.

"Okay, Jake, get washed up for dinner," he said.

As Jake trotted off, Katy murmured, "I owe you, big-time."

He cupped the back of her neck with his hand, keeping the gesture brief enough not to cross a boundary, yet long enough to supply his need for contact. "No, you don't. It's my job. And part of being a friend."

"You've done so much for us. Way more than I could have asked…I wish there was something we could do for you."

Royce released her, afraid he might make an off-color suggestion that didn't do her justice. "There is something I'd like your opinion on after dinner."

"Now you've got me curious."

"Let's eat, then." He tapped the tip of her nose with his finger. "Would you call Jake?"

Dinner was an easy affair, with Jake doing the vast majority of the talking because he was excited about his party. It gave Royce the opportunity to sit back and enjoy a good meal and good company. Why had none of his meals with Tess and Michael seemed this perfect?

Because he'd been on edge, wary that Michael might choke on his food or fall out of his booster seat. And to tell the truth, he'd been planning his escape even then. He'd been a coward, pure and simple.

"Royce?" Katy's voice interrupted his thoughts. "I asked what kind of budget you'll need for the party."

"You need budgets for that kind of stuff? Cake, ice cream, a few games and decorations. Not enough to break the bank. I can buy the supplies and you can reimburse me if you'd like."

"And invitations," Jake piped up. "We need to address those tomorrow."

"Invitations. Tomorrow. Got it." Royce was beginning to wonder what he'd gotten himself into.

Jake finished and excused himself. "I'm gonna go call Dusty and tell him about my party."

Katy and Royce worked in tandem to clear the table.

"I'll load the dishwasher later," Katy said. "Wasn't there something you wanted to discuss with me?"

"Yeah, the packet's in the front room." He collected the manila envelope where he'd left it on the coffee table.

Katy sat on the couch and turned on the reading lamp, her hair gleaming beneath the light.

Royce sat next to her and handed her the packet.

She hesitated, then opened it and scanned the pages.

Holding his breath, Royce wondered why he was on pins and needles about a relatively casual thing. But he knew—because Katy held his future in her hands and he wanted her approval.

A few moments later, she glanced up. "Looks like they'll cover a lot of your education expenses if you want to go to college or a vocational school."

"Yeah."

"Do you want to go back to school?"

"At first, I didn't think so. I'd feel funny about being there with kids half my age. But then I started thinking maybe it was a second chance for me."

She smiled. "I can understand being a little nervous about that, but you'd do fine. It seems perfect if you ask me. Any ideas where you want to go, what you want to do?"

"I'm thinking of Arizona State. There's a program for people who want to try teaching as a second career."

Tilting her head, she commented, "I've read there's a teacher shortage, so you wouldn't have a problem finding a job. Do you think you'd enjoy something like that? It's another one of those occupations that seems as much a calling as a career."

"If you'd asked me that a year ago, I would have said no. But now that I've spent time with Jake, I've discovered stuff I didn't know about myself. I'm patient, I love teaching kids how to do things and they seem to like me, too." He tried to keep the wonder out of his voice. Why had it taken so long for him to see those strengths? Or was it something that had come of the accident?

"I agree with you. You're terrific with Jake. And he listens to you."

"I'm thinking about looking into the streamlined teaching program. I've always been good with math and science and it seems like there's a need in that area. Especially in junior high."

Katy chuckled. "There's probably a good reason for that. I imagine trying to teach junior high kids is…challenging." She shuddered in mock horror. "All those raging hormones and attitudes."

"I think I can handle it. But I've been out of the U.S. for a while and I'm not up on all the ins and outs of public education. That's why I wanted your opinion."

*Liar.*

He wanted her opinion because he cared about her way more than he should.

"You've done things most of us have only dreamed about and experienced other cultures firsthand. I'm sure you could work your travels into your lectures. Real-life experience to get the kids to sit up and take notice."

"I hadn't thought of it like that." It

sounded almost noble coming from Katy. He'd simply thought of it as running away. But he was done running.

"You know, Royce, you really are a phenomenal man. I wish you saw that." Her voice was soft, her eyes deepened to almost gray.

He cleared his throat. "Thanks."

"If I didn't like the idea, would it have made a difference?"

He thought about it for a moment and shook his head. "I value your opinion, but this is something I need to do, whether anyone agrees with it or not."

"Then I think you should do it. Don't let anyone stop you." Her tone was fierce.

# CHAPTER SEVENTEEN

ROYCE HEARD FOOTSTEPS upstairs early Thursday afternoon. Surely, Jake wasn't home from school already?

Grabbing his keys, Royce locked the door and headed upstairs.

He was surprised when Katy answered the door.

"I heard footsteps and wondered if Jake forgot to tell us about an early release from school."

"I just got done with my interview and decided to take the rest of the afternoon off."

She moved inside and motioned for him to follow, closing the door behind him.

Royce studied Katy. There was an air of contained excitement about her.

"How'd it go?"

"Really well." She broke into a smile. "I think they might offer me the job."

"That's…great. Will you accept?"

"I want this, Royce. I want it bad."

He stepped close, touching her arm. "I know you do. And you really deserve it…."

The light in her eyes dimmed. "But you don't approve."

"If it weren't for the travel I'd be behind you a hundred percent. You've been gone an awful lot as it is."

She crossed her arms. "Aren't you being a little unfair? You didn't let your son stop you from pursuing your dreams."

"It probably seems that way. I just don't want to see you make the same mistakes I did. It would hurt too badly."

Katy turned away, as if unwilling to consider that he might care. "Are you saying you won't be our nanny if I take the job? I know it was only supposed to be a temporary arrangement, but I'd started to think it might turn out to be more long-term."

The thought of not being in their lives hurt worse than Royce would have imagined.

Maybe worse than watching Katy miss out on her son's life.

"To be honest, I've thought about staying on until I got my teaching degree."

The tension eased from her face. "Jake adores you and I...rely on you."

Royce ignored a pang of disappointment. He wanted more than that. How much more, he wasn't sure. "I'll be happy to stay on. But I have to be up-front and tell you there are complications."

"School? We'll find a way to work around your schedule."

"My school schedule should coincide with Jake's for the most part." He lifted her chin with his finger. "The complication I'm talking about is us. I care for you and I'm hoping you care for me."

Her eyes widened. "Of course I do, Royce. But I'm...scared. My life is so full right now and Eddie's already giving me a hard time about being involved with you even though I'm not. I'm afraid it will make things worse."

Royce had absolutely no intention of allowing Eddie to control his destiny. Katy had held him at arm's length for too long. He cupped her neck with his hand, leaning in to kiss her, long, sweetly, insistently. Then he released her.

"Royce, I—"

"I know, your life is too complicated. But I intend to change your mind. I believe what we share could be worth the complication."

KATY RETURNED HOME around noon on Saturday, secretly relieved she'd had to work a half day, thus avoiding party preparations and Royce's knowing grin.

She had tossed and turned for two nights, thinking of all the reasons she shouldn't date Royce. But she kept returning to the kisses they'd shared and how safe and cherished she felt in his arms.

Katy shook her head, figuring she should be grateful for the distraction Royce had provided. The anxiety she usually felt when thinking about birthday parties hadn't reached the extremes it typically did.

When she opened the door to her apartment, Katy walked into a gaudy display of brightly colored balloons. It was every boy's dream decor.

Jake ran up to her and said, "Hi, Mom," in a Mickey Mouse–like voice.

She took the balloon away from him. "No more helium. Where's Royce?"

"In the kitchen." He giggled.

Katy rolled her eyes and headed for the kitchen, where Royce was removing cake pans from the oven.

"That smells wonderful," she said, restraining herself from walking up behind him and wrapping her arms around his waist. It was a gesture so spontaneous, yet so foreign, it was nearly impossible to resist. And made her wonder if Royce was right. Some days they seemed like more of a couple than she and Eddie ever had.

Katy busied herself by putting out cooling racks, thus avoiding the temptation of Royce.

"Thanks." He placed the hot pans on the trays. "This is new to me. Rice Krispies Treats I can handle, but cakes are more complex. I'm going to need your assistance in the decorating department."

She held up her hands in defeat. "I'm no cake decorator. You'll have to get someone else."

"It'll be easy. Here, I'll show you the picture." He reached behind her to turn the page of a cookbook on the counter.

Katy inhaled the scent of Royce, even more enticing than the aroma of baking. His chest was against her back, sending waves of intimate messages to her brain.

"I'll do the vanilla frosting, if you do the detail work," he said, entirely too close to her ear. It sent shivers down her spine.

*What was wrong with her?*

Maybe she was trying to distract herself from worrying about the party? Or was she merely fooling herself when she thought she could resist a man like Royce? He was the real deal. Masculine and handsome, yet he knew his way around the kitchen and was a natural with her son. He might as well have been gift-wrapped for her.

"Hey, Royce, I want to frost it," Jake hopped into the kitchen like a rabbit.

"No way, slugger. This is my first cake. I get to frost it. And your mom's gonna help."

Katy brushed a lock of hair away from Jake's forehead. "You're sweaty. Have you had a bath yet?"

"Nope."

"Then go. And put on clean clothes. I washed all your favorites last night."

"Okay." He hopped away.

"Are you going to let me in on the party details?" she asked.

"I guess I can trust you with the top secret information. We're having a nice, old-fashioned party. Cake, ice cream, games like Pin the Tail on the Donkey. And then for a touch of the Southwest, a piñata on the patio. The kids really seemed to enjoy it at Chris's party."

"It sounds wonderfully normal. Not over-the-top like some parties."

"I called my dad for some hints. And my sister. I have tried-and-true, absolutely guaranteed games to please ten-year-olds."

"I'm glad to hear it. I never could have done it. And my mom had to go to the store today so she couldn't help. She might be a little late, by the way."

"Too bad she had to work."

"It might be a blessing in disguise. She's had an ax to grind with Eddie since the divorce. I guess she feels the need to protect me."

Royce grinned. "I can imagine. It took a long time for her to trust me and I'm just the Kid Wrangler. I can imagine how she'd be with someone who hurt you."

"This party may require more diplomacy than a United Nations meeting." Katy rubbed her forehead where a dull ache had formed. Her shoulders were knotted with tension. No matter how hard she tried, she simply couldn't rid herself of a deep sense of unease that had nothing to do with warring factions. She'd hoped today would prove as desensitization of sorts against her party anxiety, but she hadn't counted on strained family relationships being added to the mix.

"I'm going to change, then I'll be back to help," she said.

"Sure. I'm gonna run that last batch of balloons down to the complex clubhouse." Royce tested the outside of the cake pan on his way by. "Still hot."

"Have some patience, it takes a few minutes. You're as bad as Jake. Do I need to hide the helium from you?"

"Nah. I have traumatic memories of the

last time my voice cracked. I was about thirteen and it was humiliating."

Katy stopped. "Do tell?"

"I was thirteen and asking Marilee Hill to the junior high dance."

"You poor thing. I can imagine the scar it left. You seem to have gotten over it, though."

"I struggled with it for years. So no helium for me, thank you."

"Good."

Katy went to her bedroom and changed into a clean pair of jeans and a peasant-type blouse that brought out the color of her eyes. After freshening her makeup and running a brush through her hair, she returned to the kitchen to find the cake removed from the pans.

"How'd you manage so quickly, or shouldn't I ask?"

"With one hand? Kind of balanced it on my forearm. But don't worry, I scrubbed up all the way to the elbow."

"That's good to know." Katy realized she was actually smiling in spite of her worry. Royce was a gift, no doubt about it. Who could have known he would turn out to be the perfect person for the nanny job?

And maybe the perfect man to entice her back into the dating game?

Katy shook her head, almost wishing for some additional birthday party anxiety to distract her from the frisson of fear and excitement she felt at the prospect of getting close to Royce.

To busy herself, she did some last-minute tidying while Royce made buttercream frosting. She went back to the kitchen and watched him frost the cake.

"You're pretty good at that."

"You bet. You get the hard part, though, working with the tubes of colored frosting. I figured the baseball lacings would be pretty easy. Then you can write Jake's name."

"I know at least that much. I *have* baked his birthday cakes before."

"In the shape of a baseball?"

"No, just rectangular cakes with his name." She rested her hands on her hips. "Some of us don't feel the need to grand-stand."

"Okay, it's your turn." He finished frosting with a flourish.

"Show-off," Katy muttered. She picked up

the tube of brown frosting and made the baseball's lacings, doing a fair copy of the photo in Royce's book.

"Not bad," he commented, watching over her shoulder.

She jabbed him with her elbow. "Hey, I need room to work."

"You've got plenty of room." His breath was warm on her neck.

He picked up the frosting-laden rubber spatula and carefully placed dots of frosting down the side of her neck.

"Hey, what are you doing?" She swatted at him with her free hand, catching air.

"This," he murmured.

Katy gasped as he licked a dot of frosting from her neck. Then he kissed the next spot and trailed kisses lower.

She tried to pull away, but for some reason her body wouldn't obey the command. Instead, she closed her eyes and angled her head, enjoying the sensations radiating through her. When she thought she couldn't stand it anymore, Royce stopped.

Slowly, she opened her eyes, watching

him, bemused as he flipped over the spatula. "Wanna taste?"

"Oh, yes." She was embarrassed to realize her voice was husky.

He extended the spatula.

She intended to simply take a small taste. But somehow all sense of caution deserted her. Holding Royce's gaze, she licked the end of the spatula, taking the tip in her mouth, savoring the sweetness. And his startled expression.

"Mmm."

"That's…not nice."

Katy smiled innocently. "I don't know what you mean. Wanna taste?"

He nodded, licking his lips.

She placed the spatula in the bowl. Twining her arms around his neck, she kissed him, teasing his lips open with her tongue so they could share the deepest buttercream kiss.

## CHAPTER EIGHTEEN

THROUGH A HAZE OF NEED, Katy knew this was not a good idea. But she couldn't seem to resist the opportunity of being held by Royce.

"Mom!"

The one sound certain to gain her attention, even in the middle of a passionate kiss.

She jumped back, missing Royce's warmth as soon as she did. "Um, yes, Jake?"

"Dad was right about you and Royce, wasn't he? You're havin' sex."

Katy waited for her breathing to slow before answering. "It was just a kiss, that's all. It just…happened."

Jake folded his arms over his chest, resembling his father for a split second. Some of Eddie's attitude had obviously rubbed off. "It's my birthday party."

"I know, honey." Katy tried to remember he was just a boy. But she would definitely have to establish some boundaries. It obviously wasn't good for Eddie to be discussing her in front of Jake like that. And Jake's attitude was way too cocky.

"We got the cake decorated. See, it's a baseball," Royce said.

"Cool!" That was apparently enough to get Jake to forget about grilling them.

The doorbell rang and he headed out of the kitchen.

"Jake, you don't answer that door." Katy's hands started to shake. Her pulse raced. The fear was back again.

Royce kissed her quickly as he went by. "I'll get it."

Katy ran her tongue over her upper lip and tasted buttercream. Memories of their kiss came flooding back.

Sighing, she realized she would always think of Royce when she tasted frosting. She tidied up the kitchen and patted her mouth with a paper napkin, smiling guiltily as she did.

Then she heard her mother's voice.

She turned as her mother came into the kitchen.

"Hello, dear. The boutique was slow so they let me off early. Royce said I had to come look at Jake's cake. He said it was a team effort. And I believe he used the term *masterpiece*."

Katy tilted her head in silent question when Royce entered the kitchen, wondering whether the cake was the masterpiece, or whether he had been referring to their… teamwork. If it was the latter, Katy would wholeheartedly agree with the assessment of masterpiece.

Royce smiled innocently, but Katy knew better.

She turned her attention to the task at hand. "We better start shuffling all this down to the clubhouse. It'll take a couple trips at least."

"Not hardly. I have a plan," Royce said. He went out on the balcony and returned with Jake's red wagon. "I rinsed off the dust earlier. This will be perfect. The gifts and supplies will go in here. You can carry the cake, Audrey, and Katy can carry the piñata."

His plan worked well and before they

knew it, the cake was arranged with plates and napkins on the table in the apartment complex clubhouse. It was a separate building, connected to the office by a breezeway, and was decorated like a huge family room, with comfy couches and easy chairs in groupings designed to encourage conversation. Through an archway, there was a second room, presumably for those folks wanting quiet conversation.

A multitude of balloons and streamers had been placed throughout, making a festive statement. Katy glanced through the glass Arcadia door and noted that Royce had hung the piñata from a plant hook in the ceiling of the covered patio.

Jake stood in the center of the room, his face rapt. "It's beautiful."

Katy wrapped her arm around his shoulder and squeezed. "It sure is. You and Royce did a good job."

"Yeah, but I didn't see it all done. When's everyone gonna get here?"

Glancing at her watch, she said, "Anytime now—"

The doorbell rang.

Katy said a silent prayer, hoping it wasn't Eddie. She wasn't ready to face that particular demon yet.

Fortunately, it turned out to be Dusty and Adam, who distracted Jake. More boys arrived at intervals until it seemed the room might burst with all the pent-up energy.

"And they haven't even had sugar yet," Royce commented as he slid his arm around her waist.

She didn't have the strength to move away. Instead, she leaned against him. "You've done a terrific job. I can't thank you enough. I know how much this means to Jake."

He murmured close to her ear, "You can thank me later."

Before Katy could protest, he walked off. "Hey, boys, you want to go check out the piñata on the patio? You'll need to develop strategy for when we break it open later."

Katy smiled as she watched Royce herd the boys outside. Her uneasiness had abated and she was actually looking forward to the next couple hours.

The other children arrived and before she knew it, she was caught up in the chaotic fun.

Katy couldn't help but notice Royce's easy way with the kids and how he adroitly shepherded them through one game after the next. Pin the Tail on the Donkey was a big hit as was musical chairs, with the music supplied by Katy's MP3 player and portable speakers.

She tapped her foot in time with the music, laughing, as the children raced around in a circle. Finally, the music stopped and Dusty was left without a chair. But Royce awarded him a consolation prize and all was well.

In the end, there was one seat left for Jake and Andrew to compete to win. The music stopped and Jake was nearest to the seat. Katy held her breath as she watched the indecision flash across his face. She could tell he wanted to win so badly. And he would have, but he tripped at the end, resulting in a tie. If she didn't know better, she would have thought Jake had manufactured the tie so his guest didn't feel bad.

Glancing at Royce, she caught his attention. He nodded almost imperceptibly as if he, too, thought Jake had made a kind choice.

He clapped Jake on the shoulder. "Good job, kid."

"But I only tied. My dad says winning is better."

"Sometimes there are more important things than winning."

Jake seemed to grow taller as Katy watched the interchange. His spine grew straighter, his chest puffed out.

Katy blinked away a tear, thinking it was one of the most beautiful moments she had ever seen. And regretted, not for the first time, that Eddie wasn't half the man Royce was.

"Who's ready for cake?" Katy asked, smiling when she received a chorus of, "Me!"

Her mother came into the kitchen and helped her arrange the candles on the cake. "He's quite a man."

Katy's hand stilled. "Yes, he is."

"I had my doubts at first, but he's wonderful with Jake and the other children."

"I couldn't have asked for more." Her voice was husky.

"Do you love him?"

"Love Royce? Of course not." But she couldn't quite meet her mother's gaze. She was too confused by what she felt for Royce. It wasn't love, was it?

"Hmm. I think you're fooling yourself, but I'll let it go." She cupped Katy's face with her hand. "You deserve a good man. If Royce makes you happy, don't ever let him go. The good men are few and far between."

"I know. Eddie still hasn't shown up and he was supposed to be here at two o'clock."

Her mother snorted. "Jake might have been better off if he'd never come back into his life."

"But he has and we have to deal with it."

Royce entered the kitchen. "Have you seen Andrew?"

"No, he's not in here." Katy's voice was thin even to her own ears. Or maybe it was simply drowned out by the sound of the blood whooshing inside her head.

"I've checked both the rooms out there. But there's a supply closet, maybe he's hiding there."

"The closet, of course."

Katy started to follow him, but felt a rush of déjà vu. She remembered another party, a different closed door. Numbness took over as she followed Royce, moving as if by rote. She'd tried so hard to keep the memories at bay today, but seemed helpless to stop them.

Royce slowed to pull Adam off the back of the couch, where he rode it like a bucking bronc.

She moved past him, hesitated with her hand on the knob. Then slowly opened the closet door. Inside sat Andrew, grinning from ear to ear. "You found me. You're it."

"Yes, um, we're getting ready to have cake. You don't want to miss that."

Andrew whooped loudly and ran out of the closet to find his friends.

Royce touched Katy's shoulder. "Think maybe we ought to do the piñata before cake? You know, kids, a baseball bat, wild swinging?"

"You've got a point. You're the master of ceremonies, feel free to redirect them." Her voice was normal, not even a tremble. But inside, she was shaking. Remembering another party. And adults whispering and grabbing their children by the hand and hurrying them out the door.

Katy rubbed her wrist, where she could almost feel her mother's grip. And her mother's fear.

But she wouldn't, *couldn't* go there right now. Instead, she dedicated herself to whole-heartedly joining the party. She followed Royce into the great room, where he gathered children like the Pied Piper.

Katy continued to follow as they traipsed out to the patio, the sound of their carefree laughter drifting on the warm breeze.

The energy required to channel her attention was enormous. Thoughts of the past threatened to overtake her. And, every once in a while, Royce would glance in her direction, frowning in concern.

Blindfolded, Jake swung hard, knocking open the piñata so candy and toys spilled to the ground. The children rushed in and grabbed whatever they could get their hands on, placing their treasures in goody bags.

Her gaze met with Royce's over the tops of the children's heads. She nodded slowly, giving him the thumbs-up. His first party had been a resounding success.

He maneuvered past the children and

stood next to her. "You think they're ready for cake now?"

"I'm sure they are. Question is, are we?"

Royce laughed, the sun giving his hair mahogany glints. Glancing at his watch, he said, "Timed perfectly. Their parents should arrive about the time the sugar kicks in."

Katy held his gaze, finding comfort in the connection they shared, whether touching or not. "Spoken like a seasoned veteran. I'll go light the candles if you want to bring the children inside."

"You got it."

She started to turn, but he stopped her.

"Are you sure you're okay?"

"I'm fine." But the truth was she felt as if she might shatter. "You go round up the kids."

When Katy reached the kitchen, her mother held out Katy's cell phone. "It rang. I didn't answer it, but the display said it was Eddie. Canceling again is my bet."

Katy listened to her voice mail, not really surprised, then clicked her phone shut. "You were right. His wife is tired and having Braxton Hicks contractions. Sounds legit."

"That would be a first."

"Whether it is or not, I'm the one who will have to deliver the bad news to our son. It never gets easier."

"He's so busy, he might not even notice Eddie's missing. Here, I'll get the candles and you can dish out the ice cream."

"Thanks, Mom. I'm glad you're here." Katy was soothed by the repetitive motion of scooping ice cream and placing it on plates.

"I wouldn't miss Jake's birthday for the world."

"Even though you're not fond of birthday parties, either?"

Her mother paused, midslice. "Why would you say that?"

"Because you never let me go to one after Jenny's."

"You simply outgrew them."

Katy didn't want to call her mother a liar. But they both knew the truth and Katy was beginning to think pretending differently wasn't good.

## CHAPTER NINETEEN

ROYCE SAT DOWN in an easy chair and breathed a sigh of relief after the last child left with his parents. The party had been a blast, but once the adrenaline wore off, Royce suspected he'd want nothing more than a cold beer and the TV remote.

"Where's Dad? Is he running late?" Jake asked.

Royce glanced around. He'd been so busy with his host duties, he hadn't noticed Eddie's absence until now.

"Ask your mom. Maybe she knows."

Jake trotted off to the kitchen.

A few moments later, Royce's curiosity got the better of him and he joined them in the kitchen.

One look at Jake's tear-streaked face and he knew the news wasn't good.

"Hey, kid, what's the matter?"

"My dad's not coming at all. And I was supposed to spend the night at his house after the party."

Royce could have gladly snapped Eddie like a twig if he saw him right now. Birthdays were supposed to be carefree times when a kid was king for the day. Not some afterthought. He wondered if Michael had ever pined to have Royce there for his party. The difference with Royce was that he'd never promised to be there if he was out of country. And he'd always made sure a really cool gift arrived for Michael on his actual birthday.

But had that been enough? *No.*

"Hey, maybe we can go play some catch," Royce suggested, even though he was totally exhausted.

"Naw. I want to go to my dad's."

Audrey stepped forward and knelt in front of Jake. "Tell you what, Jake, why don't you spend the night at my condo? We'll rent some movies, pop popcorn and sleep in sleeping bags in front of the TV."

"Like camping?" Some of the spark returned to Jake's eyes.

Audrey hugged him. "Just like camping. Only without the spiders and dirt." She turned to Katy. "If that's all right with you?"

Royce's heart did a flip-flop at the tears shining in Katy's eyes. She hurt for her son.

"Of course."

He stepped close, wanting to comfort her, but unsure if she would accept it. "Why don't you and Jake go pack his bag. I'll clean up here."

"Okay. I appreciate so much all you've done today."

"I was happy to do it."

Audrey said, "It's settled, then. You go on ahead. I'll stay here and help Royce."

Katy nodded and left with Jake.

Royce worked in tandem with Audrey, hoping he wasn't supposed to make polite conversation. Though she'd thawed in recent weeks, he was still wary of the woman.

"Look at the mess on the patio!" she exclaimed. "I thought you were crazy for doing a piñata, but the children seemed to love it."

"I like to live dangerously. And what can be more dangerous than ten-year-olds hopped up on sugar, wielding a baseball bat?"

He thought Katy's mother almost cracked a smile.

"I'm sure you know I wasn't in favor of my daughter hiring you."

"Yeah, I kind of got that impression."

"It is somewhat…unorthodox. But it seems to be working out well. And Jake adores you."

"He's a good kid. The feeling's mutual."

"And how about my daughter? Is the feeling mutual with her, too?"

"Huh?" That was the most intelligent response he could find, given his surprise.

"She obviously has feelings for you. Do you return those feelings?"

After a moment's consideration, he opted for the censored truth. "She's a wonderful woman."

"She *is* a wonderful woman. And I don't want to see her hurt again. Eddie was bad enough. Be sure you don't add to her baggage."

Royce busied himself picking up paper plates and cups. It gave him the opportunity to avoid the woman's searching gaze.

He'd never stopped to think he might hurt

Katy. Somehow she seemed so self-reliant, he'd taken it for granted that she could handle herself. She was, after all, doing a pretty good job at keeping him at a distance. But he was making inroads into her resistance.

He almost smiled at the thought. Until he remembered her mother was waiting for an appropriately grave response. Which he was happy to supply because it was the truth. "The last thing I want is to hurt Katy. But thank you for reminding me what's at stake."

"Good. Because Eddie promised her the world and almost destroyed her. At least you're going into this with your eyes wide-open."

Changing the subject seemed to be best course, so he broached a question that had been bothering him. "Why do you think Eddie's back all of a sudden?"

She sniffed. "I have no idea, except that he doesn't usually think of anyone but himself. It would have been better for everyone involved if he'd just stayed under whatever rock he'd found. But it's not as if Katy can deny him the opportunity to see his son. He has visitation rights."

Royce almost winced with shame. He was really no better than Eddie. "I can see it's hard on Katy. And hard on Jake if Eddie doesn't follow through."

He lifted the trash bag out of the can and tied it.

"What's the matter?" Audrey asked. "You look awfully grim."

"Just thinking of my own son. And hoping I can make up to him all the stuff I missed when he was growing up."

She sighed. "Those times are gone for good, I'm afraid. We don't generally understand how fleeting and precious our time with our children is."

"Yeah, I guess I always thought there would be tomorrow. But I learned a little late that every day can be the last. That made me realize a lot of stuff."

"Sounds like you're ahead of the game, then. Most folks don't figure that out until they're my age or older."

Now Audrey was really starting to concern him. She was being…kind.

"Okay, Audrey, what gives? You used to hate me."

"Not hate you. I'm very protective of my daughter. You've proven yourself to be worthy of my trust."

*And worthy of her daughter?*

Even he wasn't brave enough to ask her that.

Instead, he voiced another concern. "Did Katy seem…a little uptight to you today?"

She hesitated. "Birthday parties are hard for her."

"Why?"

"That's something you should ask her."

"I have, she won't tell me."

"Then it's obviously something she doesn't want to share." The critical Audrey was back.

ROYCE WAITED FOR Katy to open the door, nudging the red wagon with his foot. There was very little left to show for the party, except a few pieces of cake and a couple of balloons. The rest of the balloons had gone home with the guests at Katy's request.

The door opened and she smiled absently. "Hey." She turned and left the door open for him to enter, a very un-Katy-like gesture.

Fatigue seemed to roll off her in waves.

He closed the door and went to her, rubbing her shoulders.

She stiffened, then leaned into his touch. "Wow, I'm even tenser than I thought."

"Yeah, I was kind of worried."

"I got through it, though."

"I thought you were even enjoying yourself. But most of the time you were wound pretty tight."

She stepped away from him. "I'll put away the cake and take the wagon outside."

"No, don't." He touched her arm. "I'll get the wagon, if you get the cake. Then you need to relax. You look like you're about ready to drop."

Katy nodded. Passing by the wagon on her way to the kitchen, she asked, "What's this?" She held aloft a bottle of wine.

"I stopped off at my place and picked that up. I thought we both could do with a glass."

"Oh, you are truly a lifesaver." She hugged him quickly and went off to the kitchen with the leftover cake and the bottle.

When he returned, the lights were low

and Katy sat on the couch, the TV on, the volume low.

"Have a seat." She nodded toward the other end of the couch. On the coffee table was a glass of wine and a piece of cake for each of them.

"We might as well sample the cake. I don't know about you, but I didn't get a bite during the party."

"Me, either." He sat down, stretching his legs out in front of him. His body hummed as if he'd worked out hard. "Who knew hosting a party could be so exhausting?"

"Your dad and sister didn't warn you?"

He laughed. "As a matter of fact, they did. But I thought they were exaggerating. I intend to call my dad tomorrow and thank him for all those parties I had."

"Jake's party had to have been a lot of hard work and I was fortunate enough to dodge most of it. You, however, weren't nearly as lucky."

"Jake seemed to have a blast and that's what counts."

"Yes." She took a sip of her wine. "Again, thank you."

"No big deal."

"I was there, remember? It was a huge deal and I can't tell you how much I appreciate what you did, what you *do* every day for Jake. He's matured since you've been around. And in other ways he's become more of a regular kid. Playing baseball, hanging out with friends. Before, I worried he might end up a loner."

Royce shifted. "He's been good for me, too. You both have."

"We make a good team, don't we? You know what the best part is? I feel like somebody has my back. The hardest part of being a single mom is feeling like the buck always stops with me. But knowing you're there gives me peace of mind."

Wrapping his arm around her, Royce marveled at the gift she'd given him. Not only a new purpose in life, but total acceptance, too. It didn't seem to matter that he might not be the man he used to be, complete with all his body parts. As a matter of fact, he suspected she might not have liked the old Royce very much. And, looking back, *he* didn't like the old Royce very much, either.

Maybe the key was accepting his past mistakes and moving forward.

His voice was husky when he said, "It's an honor to be there for you."

"You really mean that, don't you?"

"Absolutely."

Katy sighed.

"What's wrong?"

"I wish…things could be different. That my life wasn't so complex. If we'd met at a different time…"

"If we'd met at another time, it wouldn't have worked."

"What makes you so sure it would work now?"

He hesitated. "One thing the explosion taught me was that there are no guarantees. You and Jake have taught me it's worth taking the risk anyway."

Katy glanced away.

Damn, he'd said too much. Probably scared the hell out of her.

When he couldn't stand her silence a moment longer, he gently grasped her chin and turned her face so he could see her expression. The tears trickling down her face just about broke his heart. "Hey, no need to cry. Sometimes I say the wrong thing. Or say the right thing at the wrong time. Just forget I said anything."

"You said the absolute right thing to probably the wrong woman. I don't deserve all the nice things you say about me. I push you away, take you for granted. And you still come through for me every time."

"Isn't that what caring about someone is all about?"

Katy smiled a wobbly smile. "I always thought so. But I'd given up on ever finding it."

Royce tipped her chin and kissed her, gently, tenderly, trying to show her he was the kind of man she didn't think she deserved.

## CHAPTER TWENTY

KATY CLOSED HER EYES, savoring the sweetness of wine and buttercream frosting on Royce's lips—and a tenderness that made her heart ache with need. She wanted so badly to accept all that Royce offered, but she couldn't seem to allow herself, though she let him deepen the kiss.

She tried to forget that she was a woman with responsibilities and simply enjoy being a woman, to revel in the fact that this great guy wanted to be part of the whole complicated package that was her life.

Royce trailed kisses down her neck. She tilted her head to allow him better access, but her mind wouldn't turn off. She couldn't seem to stop thinking about Eddie and his threats.

Royce leaned his forehead against hers. "I better go."

"No, don't—"

"Shh. It's been a long day, we're both tired. And you seem…distracted."

"It has nothing to do with you."

"I'll accept that at face value to save my ego. Get some sleep." He kissed her on the forehead and stood.

She followed him to the door, wishing she could take him by the hand and lead him to her bedroom instead. But she was so confused, it was probably a good thing he'd suggested they end the evening. Damn. Just another way he was so in tune with her thoughts.

He opened the door and turned. "See you tomorrow?"

"Absolutely."

He nodded and walked away. She watched him until he rounded the corner, then closed the door.

Resting her head against it, Katy allowed tears to slip down her face, grieving for what she couldn't allow herself to have.

ROYCE AWOKE SUNDAY MORNING in a decidedly restless mood.

Most of the night had been spent mentally

cursing himself for being a hero. He could have spent the night with Katy, learning every inch of her body and showing her just how great they could be together—over and over again.

Still, he knew leaving had been the right thing to do. He wanted to make love with Katy more than anything, but when they did, he wanted it to happen without reservations.

But he couldn't help a flash of regret. It would have been so much nicer waking up next to her. Or on top of her...

A noise intruded on his fantasy. At first Royce thought he was imagining the tapping sound. But it came again, faintly. He knew the noise, just couldn't quite believe it.

Surely Jake wasn't home already? Checking his alarm clock, he saw that it wasn't quite 7:00 a.m.

He rolled out of bed, pulled on a pair of shorts over his boxers and padded into the front room, where the taps were more distinct, though slow in coming.

*R U up?*

Grinning, Royce grabbed the broom from the coat closet and responded.

*Jake?*

He waited, but no response.

Royce was just getting ready to repeat his question when there was a knock at his door. What the heck was the kid up to?

He opened his door to find Katy, plate in hand.

"I brought the breakfast of champions."

His mood immediately skyrocketed. He just hoped portions of his anatomy didn't do the same. "Rice Krispies Treats. My favorite. Come on in, I'll get some coffee to go with these. You're joining me for breakfast, aren't you?"

She followed him into the apartment. "Um, yes, that was my plan."

Something in her tone made him turn. "Is something going on? That's a pretty dress, by the way."

"Thank you." She smiled almost shyly and twirled.

The blue-green of the sundress matched her eyes. Her shoulders were creamy and bare, reminding him of the dream he'd been having about her sometime in the night.

"Are you going to church? Or is this a special occasion?" he asked.

"Definitely a special occasion."

Her gaze roved over his bare chest. At another time, he might have enjoyed her appreciation. But right now, he just felt…well, at a disadvantage.

"I'll go throw on a shirt while the coffee brews."

She stepped closer. "Don't. Please?"

"Um, okay."

Awareness shot through him when she reached out and placed her palm against his chest.

"I didn't sleep much last night," she murmured.

"Me, either."

Katy licked her lips, a nervous gesture that nearly sent rational thought from his head.

"All I've been thinking about is last night and how I wanted to be with you but couldn't seem to let go. I never expected this to happen with us." She took a deep breath and rushed on, "I absolutely adore you, Royce. You're the best thing to happen to me in a long time. I'm hoping maybe we can…try the whole seduction thing again this morning. If you're, um, interested?"

He didn't know how she could *not* see that he was interested.

Wrapping his arms around her, he pulled her close. "So you adore me, huh?"

She gazed up at him, smiling. "Absolutely."

"Good. Because I adore you, too."

"That's a start."

"And as far as being interested…" He slid his forearms down to her lower back and pulled her tightly to him. "Does that answer your question?"

Her smile was wide. "Oh, yes, quite nicely."

Royce kissed her deeply, the longing in his heart somehow translating through the strokes of his tongue as he nudged her toward his bedroom, never breaking contact.

Sliding her hands up his bare chest, she clung to him, murmuring his name against his mouth.

Finally, he could stand their slow progress no longer and picked her up to carry her to the bed. Moving aside his twisted sheets, he gingerly placed her on the bed, scarcely able to believe she was here, waiting for him.

Panic flashed through him. What if he couldn't make love as thoroughly as she deserved? The techniques he'd used for years might not translate to his postinjury body.

But the trust in her expression chased away his doubt. And when she reached for the hem of her sundress and pulled it over her head, all thought fled at the sight of her beautiful body. He only idly noticed the condom packets she removed from her pocket before tossing the dress to the floor.

Fortunately his shorts were easy to remove with one hand and came off in a matter of seconds, along with his briefs. "The condom might be more of a challenge."

"Not to worry." She tore open the package and smoothed the prophylactic over him.

Opening his eyes, he watched her recline and open her arms to him. Not needing a second invitation, he settled against her, resting the majority of his weight on his forearms.

"Hey," he murmured, touching his forehead to hers. "Are you sure you want to do this?"

"Positive." She rubbed her leg against his and that was all the encouragement he needed.

He rolled to the side, resting his head on his left arm so he could look and touch his fill. Skimming his fingers down the side of her breast, he smiled when she shivered.

"You're so beautiful," he whispered. "I can't believe you're here."

"I need you, Royce." She reached down to stroke him and he let out a ragged moan.

His breathing was shallow as he trailed hot kisses across her skin, her hand on him just about driving him wild. Rolling her against the pillows, he entered her.

Katy arched against him, whispering his name.

He managed to retain one last shred of sanity. "Are you okay?" His voice was hoarse.

"I won't be if you don't hurry up."

He smiled against her mouth. And made love to her as if there were no barriers between them and never would be.

## CHAPTER TWENTY-ONE

KATY AWAKENED SLOWLY, stretching languidly and coming in contact with a warm, muscular body.

*Royce.*

She snuggled close, inhaling his scent. A sense of wonder enveloped her, the perfect accompaniment to the contentment she felt. So this was what letting go was like.

She was glad she'd decided to set aside all the complications and just concentrate on her feelings for Royce.

He had become such an important part of her life that making love with him seemed like a natural extension of their friendship, their caring…their love?

The word hadn't been spoken and she was hesitant to define her emotions that closely.

Resting her head on her arm, she touched

Royce's chest, splaying her fingers posses-
sively. She'd never known things could be
this good with someone who knew her so
well. The key with Royce was that he
seemed to accept her anyway.

His eyelids fluttered open and he smiled
slowly. "Hey."

"Hey, sleepyhead."

"What time is it?"

"Not quite noon."

"Are you okay?"

Katy wished he'd quit asking her that, as
if she were some fragile doll. But then again,
it was kind of sweet having someone care
how she felt.

"I don't know, what do you think?" She
couldn't keep a straight face and broke into
a smile.

"You're still here. You haven't run from
the apartment screaming…so I guess that
means you're okay."

She stretched. "Better than okay. Much
better."

He brushed a strand of hair from her
cheek. "What we shared was pretty phenomenal for me."

"Are you fishing for compliments?"

"No. But they wouldn't hurt."

"This was…special."

He laughed. "Good thing I'm a secure guy or I'd be afraid that was a backhanded compliment."

"It's not funny, Royce. I'm being serious here. We shared something I hate trying to put into words because…it…we…"

"Were special."

"Exactly."

"In that case, *special* works just fine." He kissed her briefly, nipping her lower lip. Then he reclined against the pillow, crossing his arms behind his head. The pose screamed contented man.

Katy felt as if she wanted to share more with him. Doodling an invisible pattern on his chest with her finger, she decided to confide in him. "You've been up-front with me. Never pretended you were anything else, never pulled any punches."

"Why does this sound like a kiss-off?"

She traced his jaw with her fingers. "It's not. But I've been holding back. I haven't been willing to share everything with you."

"We shared an awful lot earlier."

Katy took a deep breath. "You've asked me about something in the past and I wouldn't talk about it. I thought I could stay protected if I didn't bring things out into the open."

"About birthday parties?"

"Yes." She wished they weren't so close at the moment, wished he couldn't seem to see straight into her heart. "My phobia about birthday parties happened after I went to a party when I was eleven."

"Jake's age."

"Yes. It was for my best friend. It started out great, very similar to Jake's—games, cake, laughter."

"So far, so good."

"There were tons of kids there. All our parents were friends, too, so many of the parents were there. When it was time for cake Jenny's mother asked me to go find her…. I looked everywhere. She wasn't in the bathroom, she wasn't in her room."

Katy felt so alone, even with the warmth of Royce's reassuring presence next to her.

He grasped her hand, twining his fingers through hers.

Her voice was shaky when she continued, "Finally, I opened the door to her brother's room. He was…doing things to her. Molesting her, though at the time I only realized it wasn't right."

"You poor kid. What did you do?"

"I told my mom. She told Jenny's mom and they got in an argument and she dragged me home."

"I'm sorry you had to go through that."

"I wasn't allowed to go to Jenny's house after that. Her parents wouldn't accept that her brother had been doing something… wrong. Our families were no longer friends, we weren't allowed to be friends. But I always wondered if I could have done something more to help her."

"You did the absolute best thing. You told an adult you trusted. Your mom did the right thing, even if Jenny's parents refused to believe you."

"That's what I try to tell myself. And most times I know it's true. I just can't stand birthday parties. They bring it all back."

He pulled her into his arms and hugged her tightly. It had felt good to get the subject in the open. It was a relief that Royce was still there for her. She felt absolutely safe in his arms. Safe enough to give in to the emotions threatening to overtake her since yesterday. Her eyes burned with unshed tears.

"Jenny…committed suicide when we were thirteen. I guess every time I go to a birthday party, I grieve all over again for her."

Royce brushed his fingertips over her cheek. "On Jenny's eleventh birthday, you lost your innocence and lost your best friend. I wish I'd known. I wouldn't have pushed for Jake's party."

"No, Jake's party was perfect and he loved every minute of it. I guess it's time I dealt with this. Maybe I have the courage now."

"You know I'll help any way I can. I'm glad you trusted me enough to tell me. It helps me understand a lot better."

He bent his head and kissed her, all the while holding her gaze, his eyes warm and loving. She felt as if they'd crossed an important bridge and could never go back. And she didn't want to.

Katy wrapped her arms around him. "I want to make love with you now that there's absolutely nothing between us."

He smiled, rolling onto his back and pulling her with him. Pressing a square packet into her hand, he said, "You read my mind. Except for one small detail."

"JAKE, ARE YOU almost ready?" Katy called. "Royce said he was coming at six, we have six-thirty reservations."

"I can't find my shoes."

She sighed in exasperation. "If I have to stop getting ready to come help you it's not going to be pretty."

Literally. Katy frowned at her reflection in the bathroom mirror. Her hair was only half-curled and the rest was frizz. Though her makeup was presentable, she suspected a pimple was about to appear on her nose.

Why was she so nervous?

Because she was having her first date with the man she was crazy about and looking anything less than spectacular wasn't an option.

To be fair, she suspected Royce wouldn't

notice a tiny blemish and if he did, he wouldn't care. The big goofball seemed to love her exactly as she was.

Katy caught her reflection smiling, with a soft, dreamy expression.

No doubt about it, she had it bad.

"You look pretty, Mom." Jake stood in the doorway. He fingered the hem of her black dress. "You're wearin' a dress and high heels and everything."

"Yes. Royce said tonight was a special occasion. Probably because it's a real date."

"Maybe he's gonna ask you to marry him."

Katy forced a laugh. "I doubt that."

What would she say if that were the case? She'd recently begun believing living happily-ever-after might just be in the cards for her.

"Royce likes you and he likes me. He should ask you to marry him."

"Please don't tell him that, honey."

"Why not? Maybe he can't think of it on his own."

"If a man can't think of marriage without help, then that means he doesn't love a woman enough to marry her."

"Oh."

Jake's glum expression tugged on her heartstrings. "You're okay with me dating Royce?"

"Yeah, Royce is the best. He never makes me feel like I'm in the way."

"You're never in the way, Jake."

"Sometimes I feel that way at Dad's house. He's always telling me to be quiet 'cause Brianna doesn't feel good. And if I ask him to do somethin' with me, he calls me selfish. That's probably why he didn't come to my party, because I was selfish."

Katy knelt next to her son and hugged him. "Oh, honey, it's not selfish to want to do things with your father. He's…"

*An asshole.*

No, she couldn't say that.

She knew that a relationship with his father was important to Jake's development, even if the guy was a jerk at times.

Trying again, she said, "Your father's got a lot on his plate right now. A new wife and a baby on the way. He's probably a little stressed out. It has nothing to do with you, sweetie."

"Do I have to stay with them every weekend?"

"No, of course not. I miss you too much."

"You do?" His face brightened. The boy wanted so badly to be wanted. And she would have given almost anything for him to have never doubted it.

"Absolutely. I want you to spend time with your dad when it works out, but I miss you like crazy when you're gone. Now, I need to curl the rest of my hair or I'm going to scare Royce."

"Nah, Royce is brave."

Katy laughed. "He sure is. Now go find those shoes. I bet they're under your bed."

## *CHAPTER TWENTY-TWO*

ROYCE LOST HIS ABILITY to speak when Katy answered the door. She was absolutely gorgeous in the sexiest little black dress he'd ever seen. Or maybe it wasn't the dress. Maybe Katy was simply the sexiest woman he'd ever seen no matter what she was wearing.

"Um, uh…"

She laughed. "Hi to you, too."

"Are you ready?" Fortunately, he'd found some semblance of a brain.

"Come in. Jake was trying to find his shoes."

"Did he look under his bed?"

"Yes."

"Wow, that means they're *really* lost."

"I'm sorry, I hope this doesn't make us late."

He shrugged. "Stuff happens. Mind if I go help him search?"

"Be my guest."

Royce went to Jake's room. "Hey. Shoes lost again?"

"Yeah. I thought they were under my bed."

"Where'd you have 'em last?"

"You sound like Mom. If I knew that, I'd know where they were."

Royce couldn't argue with his logic. Instead, on a whim he went to the closet and opened the door. There on the floor were Jake's shoes.

"Kid, I think hell officially froze over today. You put your shoes in the closet where they belong."

"Very funny." Jake grabbed the shoes and plopped his rear on the bed to pull them on. "Are you gonna ask my mom to marry you?"

Royce went very still. "Does she think that?"

"Nah. But sometimes she's pretty dense."

Royce released his breath. "I care a lot about your mom, but we're not that serious."

*Like hell.*

"Yeah, that's what she said."

Royce was unaccountably irritated by that piece of information.

"Come on. Let's go. We don't want to be late," Jake prodded.

Royce smiled, forgetting his irritation.

He drove them to a nearby steak house, complete with a few steers in a pen outside.

"Cool!" Jake exclaimed when he found out they entered the restaurant via a wooden ramp that served as a slide for braver people.

Jake scooted down without hesitation, waiting at the bottom. "Come on, Mom. It's fun."

She laughed, glancing down at her dress and heels. "Next time I'm wearing pants. I'll take the stairs tonight."

"Me, too, kid." Royce placed his hand at the small of her back, noticing how delicate Katy seemed. He'd never noticed what tiny ankles and wrists she had.

A primal wave of protectiveness came over him. Had any man threatened Katy, he would have probably broken him in half.

They were seated at a secluded booth.

Jake eyed the Western paraphernalia decorating the walls. "This is great. Do I hafta order off the kid's menu?"

"You think you can eat a whole adult meal?" Royce asked.

"You bet."

"Okay, order off the regular menu, then."

Katy flashed a smile at Royce, then turned to Jake. "I expect you to eat all your dinner, Jake. Especially if you think you're too hungry for the kids' portion. That means no dessert if you don't finish."

"Aw, Mom."

She shrugged. "It's up to you."

Royce watched the exchange. This was a mother setting limits and he needed to stay out of it.

"Okay. Kid's menu."

"Good choice, Jake."

Katy opened her menu. "You've been very secretive, Royce. What's this all about?"

"I'll wait till after we order."

The waiter came by and they ordered their food and a glass of wine in celebration. Jake got a cola with a maraschino cherry skewered by a tiny plastic sword. He was thrilled.

"Tell us, Royce. Tell us what the surprise is," Jake said. "I bet you won the lottery."

"Almost as good. Today is to celebrate a new chapter in my life. I'm officially registered for the summer session at the community college to update my core classes. I spoke with a counselor earlier in the week and he indicated I'm an ideal candidate for the expedited teaching certification at Arizona State."

"That's wonderful." Katy beamed. She turned to Jake. "That means Royce is a college student."

Jake frowned. "You don't need college. You're my nanny."

"I can do both. I'll take my classes in the morning when you're in school. Then maybe we can do some homework together in the afternoon, after we make our snacks, of course. And I can try out my teaching theories on you."

"No way. I'm not gonna be your guinea pig."

Royce and Katy laughed.

"The counselor said my job with you guys will look good on my application. I could use a reference, if you don't mind?"

Katy's cheeks turned a lovely shade of pink. He winked at her and she rolled her eyes.

But her grin was wicked when she said, "Absolutely. You do a terrific job at anything you set your mind to." She reached for his hand and said, "Seriously, though, I'm so proud of you."

"I'm kind of proud of myself. After the accident, I felt as if my life was over. That things would never be right again. Now, I've got a new job, I'm going to college and I'm going to be a teacher in a few years. It's more than I could have imagined."

Of course, he'd recently started thinking maybe something permanent might develop with Katy. He wondered if a family might be more attainable than he'd hoped.

"Did you tell Michael?" she asked.

"No, he still hasn't returned my calls." His excitement ebbed.

Katy squeezed his hand. "I'm sorry, I didn't mean to spoil your fun. I'm sure he'll be very proud of you, too."

"I hope so." He'd rather have his son's love, but his respect would be a close second.

Their meal arrived shortly thereafter.

Katy raised her glass. "To Royce. May this be only the beginning of a wonderful new life."

Jake raised his cola.

Clearing his throat, Royce said, "Thanks. It means a lot," and tapped his glass against the other two.

When they finished their meal and waited for Jake's dessert, Katy leaned forward. "I have some news myself. The Sinclair Auction House called and they want to see me in action. They've proposed a kind of trial run. There's a charity auction in conjunction with their main auction this weekend in San Diego. So they've asked me to work on a freelance basis, being a ringman and alternate auctioneer. It'll give them a chance to see how I work with one of their crews. If I'm good, it might mean I get the permanent position."

Royce didn't know what to say. He remembered what Katy had said about going after dreams and he wanted her to have the opportunity. But he was afraid she'd pay a heavy price.

"That's great. Why'd you wait so long to say something?" His tone was a little heartier than he'd intended.

"Tonight is your night, not mine. Besides, I wanted to clear it with you and Jake first. My mom has to work. Would you be willing to watch Jake while I'm gone this weekend?"

She fiddled with the stem of her wineglass, as if afraid he'd say no.

"Of course." He turned to Jake. "We can hang out together, right?"

"You bet."

"Jake, I know we haven't had a weekend together in a long time, but this is a big deal for me. Are you okay with it?"

"I'll stay with Royce. I just didn't want to go to Dad's."

Jake's statement lessened the sting of Michael's rejection. His own son might not want to see him, but Jake did. And it meant he could be supportive of Katy even if he was afraid she was making a mistake.

Royce ruffled the boy's hair. "It's a deal, then. In the meantime, I was hoping I could persuade you two to go to the movies with me tonight."

"Cool!" Jake bounced in his seat.

"Katy?"

"That would be wonderful."

"Great, I was thinking about the new Disney movie? If we hurry, we ought to be able to catch the show."

KATY TUCKED HER ARM in Royce's while they waited in the concession line. "At least let me buy the snacks. It's only fair."

"Nope. Tonight's my treat."

"You're a stubborn man."

"You're just now noticing?"

She laughed, enjoying herself immensely.

"What can I get, Mom?"

"You had ice cream at the restaurant. Popcorn would be better than something sweet."

"Can I have pop?"

She glanced at Royce and raised an eyebrow. He could be the bad guy for once.

"Sure. But, um, no candy."

Nodding her approval, Katy thought she could get used to this. They almost seemed like a family.

Katy carried the drinks and Royce carried

the jumbo-size popcorn. They chose their seats right before the lights dimmed.

Resting her head against Royce's shoulder, Katy thought she'd never been happier, even in the best of days with Eddie.

Royce leaned close, whispering against her ear. "You look beautiful tonight."

"You don't look so bad yourself."

"I'm glad we're together."

"Me, too," she murmured, tipping her face.

He kissed her, lightly at first, then with more passion.

"Mom." Jake tapped her shoulder.

She broke away. "Yes?"

"Stop it. The movie's started."

Focusing on the screen, she said, "Yes, I guess it has."

Her heart melted as she traded a knowing smile with Royce. There was the unspoken promise that they'd make love later. She didn't know how they would coordinate it so Jake didn't suspect, but somehow they would manage.

ROYCE FELT LIKE AN ASS sneaking out of Katy's apartment before dawn. Abstinence would have been the more responsible decision, but he didn't seem capable of making that unselfish choice. With Katy's sexy black dress and seductive smile at the theater, he'd been darn lucky he'd waited till two o'clock in the morning to tap on her door with their prearranged signal.

No, he'd come too far to relish the dangerous appeal of sneaking around. It simply made him feel foolish.

The time had come to make some serious decisions.

"YOU CAN JUST DROP ME OFF." Katy twisted her purse strap, nervous about her upcoming trip and all it meant to her career.

"No way. I'll park in short-term parking and Jake and I will walk you in. Won't we, Jake?"

"Yeah. Maybe I can wave at you on the plane."

"I imagine there's a window somewhere you can see out of. Before the security checkpoint."

"We'll see what we can find, okay?"

She noted how expertly he maneuvered

the SUV through airport traffic. "You're pretty good at this."

"After driving in some other countries, airport traffic is a piece of cake. I could do it with one hand tied behind my back." He grinned.

"Bad joke, Royce, really bad."

"I know, but it made you smile."

Katy was surprised to find that he was right. She rested her hand on his knee and squeezed. Mindful of Jake in the backseat, she kept her tone casual when she asked, "Have I told you lately what a great guy you are?"

What she really meant was, "I love you." The words were there, waiting to be spoken, but she seemed unable to get them out.

"Maybe. But you can always say it again."

"You are truly a great guy and I'm incredibly lucky to have you for my…friend."

"Hey, the feeling's mutual."

"I'm not stupid, I know what's going on," Jake said, leaning forward.

Katy gulped. "And what is that?"

"You and Royce like each other and want to kiss and hold hands like in the movies. But you don't because I'm here. But it's okay. I don't mind as long as no one I know is around."

Breathing a sigh of relief, she smiled at her son. "Thanks, Jake. I'm glad we have your blessing." And she really was. Because it was getting harder and harder to imagine her life without Royce.

## CHAPTER TWENTY-THREE

ROYCE PADDED BAREFOOT out of his bedroom Saturday morning, scratching his head. He grinned when he saw Jake parked on the floor in front of the TV. He cradled a bowl of cereal on his lap.

"Morning, Jake."

"Uh-huh." The boy was totally engrossed in the cartoon.

Royce went to the kitchen, starting the coffeemaker. Then he retrieved a bowl and spoon and headed back to the front room, where he set his utensils next to Jake. Grabbing a couple of throw pillows he placed them on the floor and joined the boy.

He reached in front of Jake for the cereal box, doubting the kid even noticed. "Pass the milk?"

Jake handed him the carton.

Royce settled in for his favorite Saturday-morning ritual. It was nice to have someone to share it with. Would have been even nicer if he'd known Katy was snuggled up in his bed, sated from a night of lovemaking.

When a commercial came on, Jake snapped out of his trance. "You like cartoons?"

"Yeah. The old ones are the best. Classics like the Road Runner."

Jake nodded, then discussed the merits of newer cartoons versus the classics. Conversation ended when the commercials were over.

Royce didn't remember it being like this the few times Michael had spent the night. There had been too many activities planned to simply hang out and enjoy each other's company. Maybe he'd been trying too hard to entertain the kid. Chalk up another regret. Too bad there weren't do-overs where children were concerned.

A knock at the door made him frown. "Wonder who that is so early on a Saturday morning?"

He went and looked through the peephole.

"Eddie," he said as he opened the door.

The man pushed past Royce. "Where's Katy? She was supposed to have Jake ready at eight."

"Hi, Dad."

Eddie stopped, his eyes narrowed. "Pajamas, huh? Pretty inappropriate to have the child witness your…sleepover. Go get your mom, Jake, I want to talk to her."

"She's not here." Jake resumed watching TV.

"I figured she stayed over. So she dumps the kid with you on the weekends, too?"

"I don't like your tone, Eddie. Katy never 'dumps' Jake with me. She's a very conscientious mother and taking care of Jake is my job." He crossed his arms over his chest. "Katy was called out of town for work. When did you talk to her about the change in plans?"

"She's gone an awful lot. It can't be healthy for Jake."

The guy had a lot of nerve, especially considering how long he'd been absent from Jake's life. Royce tried to remain calm. For Jake's sake. "You didn't answer my question. When did you talk to Katy?"

"Earlier in the week. But I left a voice mail last night telling her I'd changed my mind and wanted to pick up Jake at eight this morning."

"So you didn't actually talk to her?"

"No. But I gave her plenty of notice."

Royce disagreed, but he didn't think it was his place to get in the middle. "Maybe you and Katy can sit down and clarify the ground rules when she gets back."

"That's none of your business. I'm here now and I'll take my son. Jake, get your things, we're leaving."

Jake turned, frowning. "How come?"

"Because I said so."

"Wait a minute. Katy is my employer and I'm responsible for Jake's welfare. He's not going anywhere until I confirm it with her."

Eddie stepped forward, crowding Royce. "He's my son, not yours. He'll come with me."

Royce resisted the urge to head-butt the little weasel. "Get out of my face, Eddie. I haven't had my coffee yet and you're starting to get on my nerves."

Apparently something in Royce's expression must have convinced the other man he was serious.

Eddie backed up a few steps, running his hand through his hair. "Hey, man, I'm between a rock and a hard place. Brianna says I gotta prove I can be a good dad before the baby's born or she's outta there. She thinks I'm blowing off Jake like last weekend."

Ah, his wife had been the reason. Eddie didn't want a relationship with Jake because he'd suddenly realized what he was missing, but because he saw it as a way to keep his wife. Royce's heart ached for Jake, who seemed oblivious. But Royce knew from experience the kid could be listening intently while he seemed to be in another world.

"Why don't I try to call Katy now?" Royce offered.

"I'd appreciate it. Maybe she'll pick up for you."

Royce got his cell and called Katy. It went to voice mail. "Hey, Katy, it's me. Call me as soon as you can. Everything's okay with Jake, just need to clarify something."

He turned to Eddie. "Voice mail. How

about if I bring Jake to your place if Katy gives the official okay? That would probably square things with your wife, wouldn't it?"

"I hope so." Eddie headed toward the door. Almost as an afterthought, he called, "I'll see ya after your mom calls, Jake."

Jake didn't glance up from the TV. "Uh-huh."

Royce was relieved Jake didn't seem to mind, because he'd just remembered the boy hadn't wanted to go to his father's this weekend. What a mess. Royce didn't envy the tightrope Katy had to walk.

He resumed his position on the floor, eyeing his soggy cereal with disgust. "Hey, Jake, what d'ya say we go grab a couple breakfast sandwiches and head to the park for a game of catch?"

"When this show is over?"

"Yeah, when this show is over."

"Cool."

Royce patted him on the back, wondering if maybe there was such a thing as karma. He'd screwed things up royally with his own son and yet, he was able to be here for Jake now that Eddie was screwing up.

KATY BARELY HAD TIME to grab a granola bar Saturday morning before she was thrown into last-minute preparations for an unfamiliar auction house. Her stomach protested. She only hoped it didn't growl in the middle of the auction. She used a wireless mike and lived in fear it would amplify the sound.

It was midafternoon the next time she was able to take a break. She removed her cell phone from her purse and swore under her breath.

She'd missed several calls from Eddie and one call from Royce. They had to have come in after she'd talked to Jake last night.

The first message made her angry. Eddie wanted to change plans for the weekend and expected her to have Jake ready at eight. How like him to think she'd drop everything. How like him not to consider she might have plans. And how like him to be annoyed when everyone didn't comply with his plans.

Then she got to Royce's message. It had her panicking until it finally sank in that he'd said nothing was wrong.

When she reached him, he sounded a bit rough around the edges.

"Eddie was pretty pissed," he said. "I wouldn't let him take Jake unless you okayed it."

"I didn't get his message till just now. He must've called after I talked to you and Jake last night. I guess it's okay if he goes to Eddie's. I'm not thrilled about the last-minute change in plans, but I don't want anyone to think I'm being uncooperative."

"Maybe you two could sit down and hash out some ground rules when you get back?"

"It's all there in our child custody documents, but, of course, he probably wouldn't read those."

"You, um, might want to talk to Jake when you get home. I think he may have heard Eddie talking about him." Royce related his conversation with Jake's father.

Katy sighed. Her heart contracted at the thought of Jake being disappointed yet again by his father. He deserved so much better. "How's Jake doing?"

"Pretended he didn't hear. But he's been moody and hyper all afternoon."

"That's not like him unless he's upset about something. I knew I shouldn't have come this weekend, but it was just such a terrific opportunity."

"You had no way of knowing this would happen."

"You sound tired."

"I am. I've tried to keep Jake busy so he wouldn't think about his dad. We've played catch, video games, board games, you name it. We're gonna go hike South Mountain in a few minutes."

"Maybe it'll be a good thing for Eddie to have Jake this evening. Maybe he can mend some fences with his son and you'll have a chance to rest."

Royce sighed. "I was so much younger when Michael was this age. I don't remember him being this exhausting."

"Imagine how your ex felt. She had him 24-7."

"I don't need you to remind me I wasn't there for my son." His tone was sharp.

"I didn't mean it that way." Or did she? Maybe she wanted him to think about what it was like to be there every single day.

To see if he was up to parenthood for the long haul.

"Sorry, I'm just tired. And maybe a little sensitive about the whole Michael thing. He still hasn't returned my calls."

"I'm sorry, Royce. You deserve the chance to make it right. Maybe you should just fly out to see him at one of his races."

"It's a thought. I better get going if I'm gonna follow through on my promise to Jake about that hike. Then I'll drop him off at Eddie's place."

"Thanks, Royce… I miss you."

"Yeah, I miss you, too. Talk to ya later."

Katy was vaguely disappointed with their conversation. Sure, she was grateful Royce seemed to be handling the situation with Eddie and taking care of Jake. But it would have been nice if he'd asked about the auction.

Sighing, she decided she just wasn't used to the give-and-take of a relationship. Did she expect too much?

ROYCE NORMALLY ENJOYED hiking South Mountain, but that was when he wasn't with a ten-year-old who insisted on going off the trail, poking at snake holes and throwing rocks over the edge.

"Come on, Jake, cut the crap. Can't you just stay on the trail and stay out of trouble?"

Jake threw a stick over the edge and Royce hoped like crazy it didn't hit someone on the trail below. He grabbed Jake by the arm. "Enough."

"You don't have to be so mean."

"I'm not being mean. I want you to behave and you're not listening to me."

Jake's chin came up. "I don't have to listen to you. You're not my dad."

"Is that what this is about? You're mad at your dad so you're taking it out on me?"

"I'm not mad. I'm just havin' fun."

Royce was dangerously close to losing his temper. "You are endangering yourself and other people and I won't allow it. Now, hike in front of me so I can keep an eye on you."

Jake threw him a dirty look, but complied—for one minute before running up a boulder-strewn trail. The kid had to be half mountain goat.

They made it to the top and Royce tried

to enjoy the view. The harsh beauty of rock formations and cacti gave way to red-tile roofs below.

Inhaling deeply, he felt his tension start to ease.

"See, wasn't this worth the climb?" he asked.

"It's boring."

Royce sighed. He'd never seen Jake behave like this before. It was as if the child was intentionally trying to antagonize him. The whole Jekyll and Hyde routine had to be the result of overhearing Eddie practically admit he was being forced to see his son.

With that in mind, Royce attempted to be more understanding. "It was better than hanging around the apartment."

"I'd rather watch TV. Besides, you're just going to dump me at my dad's house."

"Jake, I'm not dumping you anywhere. I have to take you to your father's house because it's the right thing to do. It's what the courts want and your mother could get in trouble for not complying."

"You're just being my friend because my

mom pays you." There was so much hurt and anger in Jake's voice, Royce stepped closer, putting his arm around the boy's shoulder.

"I'm your friend whether your mom pays me or not."

"I don't believe you." Jake knocked his arm away. Then he turned and started down the trail.

"Jake, wait—"

But Jake broke into a run.

Royce followed at a jog, but slowed to pick his way down the rocky slope.

He could see Jake gaining momentum.

"Jake, stop!"

But the boy couldn't or wouldn't slow his pace. He jumped boulders and slid on loose gravel, widening the gap between them.

Royce clambered faster, ignoring the fact that one wrong step could lead to a twisted ankle, or worse, a fall.

Royce panicked when Jake went around a sharp turn in the trail and he couldn't see him anymore. Breaking into a run, the only thing he cared about was reaching Jake before he did something stupid.

He rounded the curve in the trail, his breath coming in short, tortured gasps.

He was too late.

JAKE TRIED NOT TO CRY, but his arm hurt like crazy. "Royce. Come get me."

He'd been jumping from boulder to boulder but then he'd jumped and there hadn't been another boulder, just air.

He looked up to see Royce's face. It was the only time he'd seen Royce act scared.

"It's okay, kid. Just lie still and I'll come get you."

"Hurry." He wiped his hand across his eyes.

Royce scrambled down the slope, dislodging gravel and small rocks that skittered downward. "Are you okay?"

"My arm hurts."

Royce got a funny look on his face. "I should call the paramedics."

"No! Just take me home."

"I can't do that, buddy. You're going to need a doctor for that arm."

He opened his cell phone. "No service. If I go toward the top I can—"

"No, don't leave me."

Royce stood there, as if he didn't know what to do. Weren't grown-ups always supposed to know what to do? Jake's arm hurt and he wanted his mom.

Jake said, "Help me up to the trail. I can make it from there."

"I don't know—"

"Please, Royce? You can do it."

"Okay. Can you tuck your hurt arm up close to your body?"

Jake complied, only crying out once.

Royce picked him up and carried him up the slope. Though every step sent pain shooting up his arm, it didn't seem nearly as far with Royce carrying him.

Jake knew he should have tried to walk himself, but he felt safe. Hiding his face in Royce's shoulder, he hoped Royce didn't get tired of him being a big baby. Or get mad at him for being a pain in the butt earlier.

Jake had just been so mad at his dad that all he'd wanted to do was run away or throw something.

ROYCE STARTED TO SHAKE the minute he got Jake settled in the SUV. His only thought was getting the boy to the hospital as quickly as possible.

He drove like a man possessed, glancing at Jake to make sure he was still conscious. How could he have let this happen?

All the fight seemed to have gone out of the boy and that's what worried Royce the most. His face was tearstained, his eyes full of pain.

"You hanging in there?"

"Yeah. I'm sorry, Royce. I should've listened."

"Hey, we'll be at the hospital in a minute and they'll fix you up good as new."

When they got there, Royce barely had the SUV in Park before he was by Jake's side, gently lifting him.

Royce's heart contracted when Jake cried out in pain. He broke into a jog as he carried Jake into the Emergency Room. Depositing him carefully on a chair, he said, "I've got to go fill out some paperwork with that lady over there."

"You're not gonna leave, are you?"

"Not a chance."

Royce went to the admitting counter and

gave the appropriate information. He removed Jake's insurance card from his wallet, thanking God that Katy had insisted that he carry the extra card, along with her written permission to administer medical care.

When the administrator asked how the injury happened, Royce told her the abbreviated version.

She raised an eyebrow. "Why weren't the paramedics called?"

"There was no cell service and Jake didn't want me to leave him and it was...just easier to bring him myself."

"You shouldn't have moved him. He could have spinal injuries."

Royce's blood went cold. "I—I didn't hurt him, did I?"

The woman's lips thinned. "We won't know that until a doctor sees him."

Royce felt as if the floor had dropped from beneath him. He loved Jake and had only tried to do what was best. But he'd screwed up big-time. Real parents didn't screw up that way. Real parents like his ex-wife, Tess. And Katy.

He'd always worried he didn't have what it took to be a parent when the going got tough. It seemed now that he was right.

KATY RECEIVED A CALL ten minutes before the auction was set to start and she was trying to quell her nerves. It came through on the house phone.

"Hello."

"It's Royce."

"I'm so happy to hear from you." Her heart swelled. He was such a great guy, calling to give her encouragement right before her big night. "I'm a little nervous. Kind of like stage fright."

"I wouldn't bug you unless it was important." His voice was tense.

"Oh." She was disappointed, then alarmed. "What's wrong? Has something happened to Jake?"

"I'm sorry, Katy, I should have kept a better eye on him. He fell while we were hiking South Mountain and I think his arm's broken. He might have a concussion, too. And, um, they said he shouldn't have been moved, but I couldn't get cell service so…I just brought him in myself. There's been a pileup on U.S. 60 and I don't know when they'll get to us."

Katy's pulse pounded. "But he's going to be all right, isn't he?"

"He seems fine except for the arm. He's in a lot of pain. I'm really sorry, Katy."

"I'm sure it's not your fault. I feel so horrible that I'm not there. Have they given him anything for the pain?"

"Nope. Not until the doctor sees him. He's been a real trouper but that's starting to wear thin. He seems to want me to stay close. But I called Eddie and he's on his way. Not necessarily happy about it, but on his way."

Katy started to pace, scraping her hair away from her forehead. She should be there for her son. "He's never been in the E.R. before and I'm sure he's scared. I should be there. You'll stay even after Eddie gets there, won't you? Jake trusts you, knows he can depend on you. Even if I leave now, I can't be there for a couple hours."

Realizing she was babbling in panic, Katy took a deep breath.

Royce's voice was oddly detached when

he said, "Katy, Eddie is his father. Once he gets here, Jake won't need me."

It sounded as if he was ready to bolt for the door the second Eddie arrived.

Katy stifled a moan, wishing she were in Phoenix taking care of her son and not having to depend on others to do it. And this was *not* the Royce she'd grown to love and depend on. Now, when she needed him most, he seemed almost afraid.

"Let me talk to Jake."

"Here he is."

"Mom?" Jake sounded so young and scared. His usual bravado was absent from his voice.

Katy wiped tears off her cheek. Clearing her throat she said, "It's me, honey. It sounds like you banged up your arm pretty good."

"Royce says I may get a cast."

Closing her eyes, Katy willed herself to be calm. It would only scare Jake if he thought she was afraid. Fortunately, her voice didn't tremble when she said, "That'll be cool. You can have the other kids sign it."

"But it hurts, Mom. Really bad." Jake started to cry and it tore her heart out.

What was she doing hundreds of miles away when her son was hurt and scared? She didn't know how much longer she could keep Jake from realizing how upset she was.

"Royce says your dad is on his way. Do you think you can hang on till I get there, honey? If I leave right after the auction, I can catch the last flight."

"I want you here now."

"I know you do. And I want to be there with you so bad. But I made a commitment. I can't simply leave."

"Your boss'll understand."

"Jake, put Royce back on, okay? I love you, honey, and I'll be there as fast as I can."

She heard the phone being shuffled in the exchange. Royce came on the line. "Katy, Jake needs you. How soon can you get here?"

Katy felt torn in too many directions and unable to come up with a satisfactory solution. So she did the best she could and prayed it would be enough.

"I'm nearly five hundred miles away and the auction is about to begin. Believe me, I'll get to the airport as fast as I can after the auction. If I don't go back to the hotel for my luggage, I can probably catch the last flight out and be there by midnight."

"What if I can't handle it?" His voice was uncharacteristically tight.

"What's going on, Royce? This isn't like you."

"I'm not the guy you want around when there's a sick or hurt kid. It's just…not my thing."

Something in the way he said it reminded her of Eddie. She felt a wave of anger, a welcome relief after guilt and heartache. "You can't just pick and choose when you're a parent or stepparent. You've got to be there for the good times *and* the bad. Jake needs you right now. *I* need you right now."

There was silence.

"Royce?"

"I never said I wanted to be a stepparent, Katy. I thought I could do this, I really did. I guess I was wrong."

## CHAPTER TWENTY-FOUR

KATY SAT AT THE AIRPORT. Her flight home was delayed due to repairs. Glancing at her watch, she tried to be patient. As long as she could get out tonight, everything would be fine.

She flipped open her cell and called Royce again. And again, it went into voice mail. Had he left Jake alone? Or, almost as bad, alone with a father who couldn't always be counted on?

Calling information next, she jotted down the number for the hospital. Then she called, identified herself and asked for Jake's status. The nurse politely told her they didn't give out status reports over the phone due to privacy laws.

Frustration started her pacing. "Can you tell me if Royce McIntyre is with my son? He's Jake's…nanny."

She received the same answer about privacy laws.

"Could you at least page Royce McIntyre for me? He's not answering his cell."

Katy was on hold for what seemed like an eternity. Finally, the easy-listening music clicked off and the nurse came back on. "I'm sorry, ma'am, he's not answering the page."

"Thank you."

Katy felt totally helpless, cut off from her son when he needed her. She should have never come here. One thing was for sure, because she'd bailed only moments before the auction, she wouldn't be getting a second chance. But as soon as she'd finished talking to Royce, Katy had realized there was no way she could concentrate on an auction if she was worried about Jake.

ROYCE THOUGHT he might pass out when they set Jake's arm without anesthetic, the boy's pain cutting him to the core.

*It's just a job, it's just a job.*

But no matter how many times he told himself, he knew the truth and the panic started all over again. This was the reason he'd never made it as a full-time dad.

Eddie came around the curtain a few minutes later.

"Dad!"

"Hey, Jake." Eddie went over to the bed, but didn't get too close. He eyed Jake as if he might have something highly contagious.

"I have a cast." Jake raised his arm.

"Yeah, I see that. Looks like you're doing okay."

"It hurt really bad. Especially when they set it a few minutes ago."

"Yes." The nurse bustled in. "I heard you were really brave. I've got some medication for you to take that'll help with the pain." She handed Jake a cup of water and a pill.

"You couldn't have given that to him before the doctor set his arm?" Royce asked drily.

"You'll have to talk to the doctor about his reasons. I imagine it had something to do with ruling out nerve damage."

Royce closed his eyes, willing away the nausea. Had he done something to damage Jake's nerves? He would never forgive himself.

He felt a touch to his arm and opened his eyes.

"He's going to be fine," the nurse assured him.

Royce cleared his throat. "Thank you."

She smiled and patted his arm, as if he were any run-of-the-mill nervous father, instead of a major screwup. Then she showed Jake the call button and told him to ring if he needed anything.

Royce turned to Eddie. "What took you so long?"

"I got here as soon as I could." But he avoided Royce's gaze. "Brianna's been having premature contractions and I needed to make sure she was taken care of before I left."

That's what Eddie had said when he missed Jake's birthday party.

"Well, you're here now, that's what matters. I figured I'd shove off…."

Jake grasped his hand. "No, Royce, don't go. Please, stay with me?"

"Your dad's here now. You'll be fine."

"Please, Royce?"

Royce didn't have the heart to disappoint him. "Okay, but only for a little while."

"Does Katy know?" Eddie asked.

"I called her right after I called you. Her auction was about ready to start and she intended to catch the last plane out afterward."

"That's damn nice of her. You'd think she'd drop everything with our son hurt."

"Don't say that, Dad. Mom wanted to be here. But she made a commitment for the auction and needed to see it through."

Eddie muttered something under his breath about Katy being selfish.

"She has a career, Eddie. One that feeds, clothes and keeps a roof over their heads. It's not always an easy choice," Royce said, even though it had been easy for him when Michael was growing up. And apparently Eddie had no problem choosing when Brianna wasn't on his case about proving he was a good father.

Eddie shook his head. "Boy, are you gonna be in trouble when she gets back."

Royce was tempted to wipe the smirk right off his face. "Why do you say that?"

"You let her baby get hurt. She'd skin me alive, but I guess maybe she has reasons for keeping you intact."

"Can it, Eddie. You need to remember she's Jake's mother and watch your mouth." He angled his head in the boy's direction.

"Yeah, well I'm sure it's no worse than what she says about me."

"Katy would never say anything bad about you in front of Jake. You owe her the same courtesy. Kids are smart. They figure out what's what pretty quickly."

"Good, then he'll see you for what you are soon. A crippled guy looking to feel whole again and using my ex-wife and son to do it."

Royce's blood pressure went up a few notches and there were a number of cutting remarks he wanted to make. Not to mention the desire to show Eddie how little the term cripple applied to him. But a shred of doubt crept in. Was that what he'd done? Tried to use Katy and Jake to feel whole again?

He gently disengaged Jake's hand from his. He could not, *would* not get involved in this mess. "I'm gonna go for a walk, kid. I'll be back."

"Don't leave!"

Royce hesitated, then squared his shoulders and walked out the door, telling himself

Jake didn't need him. And hating himself for being such a coward.

"FINALLY!" KATY EXCLAIMED. "Why haven't you answered your phone, Royce? I've been calling and calling. They wouldn't tell me a thing about Jake."

"I had to turn off my cell in the E.R. Sorry, I should've called you." But he didn't sound sorry. He sounded…distant.

"Are you guys home yet?"

"Not exactly. I'm…stretching my legs outside."

"Are they admitting him?"

"I don't know. I don't think so. Eddie's there. When's your flight get in?"

"Ten tomorrow. I'm back at the hotel. The last flight out was canceled due to mechanical problems. I might as well have conducted the auction."

"You didn't?"

"No, I was too worried about Jake. I figured I'd hang out at the airport and hope for a standby. The second-to-last flight turned out to be overbooked. Then the last flight was canceled."

"What'd the auction people say?"

"They were pretty angry and I don't blame them. But my son had to come first."

Royce cleared his throat. "I admire that kind of dedication, Katy. It was pretty hypocritical of me to give you a hard time earlier."

"Why?"

He seemed to ignore her question, saying, "But I don't think I'm wired for the kind of parental dedication I expected from you. You came through, I didn't."

Katy scraped her hair off her face. "What are you saying?"

"Nothing I want to get into now. Maybe both of us were just seeing what we wanted to see. I got hit by a big dose of reality today."

"I know it's been rough and I'm so glad you were there for Jake. It'll be better when I get home." She hated the desperation in her voice. He couldn't bail on them.

"I'm not so sure. Maybe we rushed things. It might be a good idea to cool it for a while."

"You're getting cold feet."

"It's not cold feet. It's being realistic about my history, my personality. Like I said, we can talk about it later. I just want a peaceful evening and time to think. I'm going home. Eddie can handle it, Katy. It might even give him a chance to bond with Jake."

"Royce—"

The connection went dead. She could try calling him back, but knew he wouldn't answer.

Katy sat down on the bed in her generic midrange hotel and cried.

ROYCE HATED HIMSELF as he drove home. Not because he'd left. But that he'd gone back on a promise to Jake. He'd promised to return and he'd bolted instead.

Royce had always prided himself on the fact that he was up-front in his dealings with women and kids. He never promised more than he could give so he never had to go back on his word.

At least that had been his goal since he'd left Tess and Michael when his son was still a toddler.

Now, he didn't even have that.

His cell rang as he pulled into a parking space at the apartment complex. He almost didn't look at the display, figuring it was Katy again. He simply couldn't deal with her right now.

But when he checked, he couldn't help but grin.

"Michael, how's it going?"

"Good, Dad. I got your calls. There was something important you wanted to talk to me about?"

"Yeah, I did. I do. But not over the phone. Maybe I can fly to meet you next weekend?"

"How about if you come pick me up at the airport in Phoenix? Maybe we could grab a bite to eat and get caught up?"

"You're here? Now?"

"Yep. No races on Mother's Day weekend, so I thought I'd fly in and we could get caught up. I'll take the red-eye right back out, so I can spend Mother's Day with Mom. But that at least leaves us a few hours."

Royce closed his eyes, almost unable to comprehend his good fortune. He could finally tell his son what was in his heart.

"I'll pick you up in half an hour. What terminal are you in?"

He wrote down the information on a

receipt stuffed in the console, afraid he might forget in his eagerness.

Putting the SUV in Reverse, Royce decided the day had gone from bad to wonderful in a matter of seconds.

As he was nearing the airport, his cell rang again. Afraid it might be Michael, he pulled into a parking lot to answer. It was the hospital.

"Royce, when're you coming back?"

"Sorry, kid, something came up." That at least was the truth. "Your dad can take you home."

"He left."

"What? He's coming back, isn't he?"

"I don't think so." Jake's voice was small and scared. "His wife called and said the baby was comin'."

Royce covered the speaker and swore.

"Is my mom coming?"

"Not till tomorrow morning. She couldn't get a plane out tonight."

"I'm scared."

"There's nothing to be afraid of." Royce was horrified that Jake was alone in the hospital with nobody to take him home. He never would have left if he'd known Jake would be all by himself. But who was he fooling? He'd left him with Eddie and he'd known Eddie wasn't reliable.

Royce knew he had to make it right, no matter how uncomfortable the situation was. He might not be the best guy to handle injured kids, but for Jake, at this moment, he was the *only* one. But how could he be in two places at once? There were two people he cared about depending on him. Two boys who both deserved apologies.

Royce could have kicked himself. Katy must have felt similar conflicting loyalties and he'd simply heaped more worry on her because he was afraid.

"Royce?"

"I'm here, Jake. Tell the nurse I'll be there as soon as I can. I will absolutely be there for you."

"Thanks, Royce. You're the best."

The boy's eagerness made Royce feel like a total jerk.

"It's gonna be an hour or so, though." He calculated quickly. This might be his only opportunity to make things right with

Michael. "I've got to pick someone up at the airport."

"I can wait."

"See ya in a little while, kid. Give the nurses my cell number if they need to confirm that I'm picking you up."

How in the world was he going to explain this to Michael? His heart sank when he realized he'd be juggling two emotionally charged situations at one time.

KATY GRABBED THE KEYS from the attendant's hand and got in the driver's seat. "You're sure this is the fastest one you've got?"

"Yes, ma'am. Are you sure you don't want to take the extra insur—"

Starting the ignition, Katy peeled out of the parking lot and headed east. If she hadn't been so worried about Jake, she might have laughed aloud for the sheer joy of having all those horses at her disposal.

Instead, she watched the road ahead and thought only about being with her son.

## CHAPTER TWENTY-FIVE

ROYCE JOGGED into the baggage claim area, glancing around.

"Dad." Michael moved forward, his stride athletic and assured.

Again, Royce was shocked to realize his son was a grown man.

"Michael." Royce extended his hand, then pulled his son into a hug. His eyes burned. He stood back.

"You look good, Dad." Michael's gaze rested only briefly on Royce's left arm. "A hell of a lot better than the last time I saw you."

"I imagine I looked pretty rough in that hospital."

Michael nodded.

Royce would have liked to have taken this visit slowly, but it seemed like everything needed to happen at warp speed or the plan might disintegrate into chaos.

"No bags?"

"Nope, pretty much a turnaround trip. I traveled light." He slung a backpack over his shoulder.

"I'm so glad you made the trip. Car's this way." Royce all but herded him toward the exit.

"Hey, where's the fire?"

"Damn. I've imagined so many times how this visit would go and it definitely wasn't like this. I, um, kind of promised I'd pick someone up at the hospital. If there were any other way, I would have said no. But I couldn't just leave him there…."

"Okaay. I'm not sure what I expected but this wasn't it. I thought we could go someplace quiet and talk."

"Me, too, kid. Me, too. Let's just make the best of it, okay?"

Michael shrugged. "Sure. I'm used to second place with you."

"Ouch. I had that coming, though. That's the reason I wanted to talk to you." He longed to stop, take a deep breath and remember all he'd intended to say. "You deserve my undivided attention when I talk to you. But I'm afraid this may be my only—"

Royce's cell rang. He pulled it from his pocket.

"Yeah, Jake." His tone was more curt than he intended.

"I told the nurse you were coming. When're you going to get here?"

He glanced at his watch. "Half an hour, okay, kid? Hang in there, it won't be much longer."

Royce clicked his phone shut. "Where were we?"

"Where we've always been. Me wanting something from you that you just can't give. And you totally clueless about what it means to be a father. This was a mistake. I'll just get a return flight."

Royce grabbed his son's arm. "Michael, no. This is important. I've thought and thought about it ever since I got back to the States. Actually, since I woke up in Germany and saw you standing by my bed, all grown-up."

Indecision flashed in Michael's eyes.

"Please? It may not be a Hallmark father-and-son reunion, but we'll make it the best we can."

Michael sighed. "I've come this far, I might as well hang out with you on the way to the hospital."

"Thanks, son. I know I don't deserve second chances. Your mother raised you to be one heck of a man."

"Yes, she did. She said to tell you hi, by the way."

"She's a good woman. How's her new family?"

"I've never seen her happier. Sam's a great guy."

"I sent a wedding gift."

"Mom mentioned it. I think it meant a lot to her."

Royce nodded, not knowing what to say.

They left the terminal and headed toward short-term parking. Michael's athletic stride ate up the asphalt, whereas Royce'd had a long day. But he managed to meet him, stride for stride.

"Here's my SUV. You want to drive?"

Michael grinned. "I'm not familiar with the city. Otherwise, I'd accept and turn your hair gray."

Chuckling, Royce said, "I certainly don't need any more of that. Toss your stuff in the backseat."

They settled in and Royce piloted the SUV through the airport traffic lanes. Fortunately, it wasn't busy this time of night.

Once they reached the freeway, Royce breathed a sigh of relief. He might just be able to pull this off.

"So who are we picking up at the hospital?"

"His name's Jake. I've got a job as his, um, nanny."

Michael laughed. "Yeah, Mom told me, but I didn't believe her. You have to be one of the least kid-friendly people I know."

Michael's words stung. "You and I always had a great time."

"Yeah, as long as I didn't get sick, hurt or scared. Any of those things happened and you couldn't drop me off at Mom's fast enough."

Royce scratched his head. "I don't remember it quite like that, but you could be right."

"That's why I didn't spend the night until I was about twelve. You didn't do nightmare detail. And if I ate too much junk and threw up, you'd bundle me in the car with a barf bowl and take me home."

"That happened once."

"Once was enough. You got your point across. No weakness allowed."

"I'm sorry." His voice was husky. "I was a real jerk. I missed out on so much and I really let you down as a father."

"Yeah, you did."

Royce was proud of the way Michael admitted the facts but without anger or bitterness.

"It was never your weakness I was afraid of. It was mine…. I know I can't ever make up for what we've lost. But I'd kind of like to start over. Maybe we can still have some sort of relationship?"

He waited, the silence making his heart pound.

"I don't know, Dad. I don't know."

Releasing a breath, he said, "Okay, fair enough. Can we play it by ear?"

"Yeah. That's all I can do."

JAKE TRIED HARD to be brave, knuckling tears from his eyes. No need to cry. Royce would be here.

But Royce had already promised to come back and hadn't.

Then his dad left to go help his wife have the baby.

And his mom couldn't get here from California until tomorrow.

Jake was all alone.

Then two men entered the room and he knew everything would be all right.

"Royce!" He launched himself at the man.

Royce caught him midleap and gave him a bear hug, before setting him on his feet. "I'm here, Jake."

Jake peeked around him to the other guy. "Aren't you—?"

"Michael McIntyre." The famous stock-car driver shook his hand as if he was a grown man.

"Cool."

"Michael, this is Jake Garner."

"Nice to meet you, Jake."

"Wow, I'm really gonna have some stories to tell at school on Monday."

"Would you like me to autograph your cast?"

"You bet." Jake forgot all about the pain and the time he'd been alone. "You got a pen, Royce?"

"I carry one for times like these." Michael pulled a marker from his pack and signed Jake's cast with a flourish.

"I've filled out all the discharge paperwork as your mom's representative, so we're ready to get out of here. What're the chances I might treat you guys to a late dinner? Or early breakfast, however you want to look at it?"

Michael ruffled Jake's hair. "I'm up for it if you are, Jake."

"I'm starving. Let's go." He grabbed Royce's hand as they walked out the door, then dropped it when he caught Michael eyeing them. He didn't want Michael McIntyre thinking he was a total baby.

ROYCE WAS AMUSED when both Michael and Jake opted for breakfast, ordering tall stacks of pancakes and polishing them off in record time.

They talked about Michael's racing career and Jake's elementary school social world.

"I just turned eleven. I had this big birthday party with cake and ice cream and a piñata. Royce did it all, even baked the cake."

Michael stiffened. "He did?"

"Yep. It was really cool."

"I bet it was. Of course, I wouldn't know. He didn't make it to many of my birthday parties."

"He didn't?" Jake frowned, glancing at Royce for confirmation.

"I was working out of the country most of the time."

Jake nodded, as if satisfied with his response.

Michael shrugged.

This was so difficult, trying to make amends to Michael without totally disillusioning Jake in the process.

But he had to try.

"See, Jake, I did some pretty stupid stuff when Michael was growing up. I worked overseas instead of being there for my son. It's something I really regret."

"You should have been there for birthdays and stuff," Jake commented.

"Yes, I should have."

An uncomfortable silence descended and Royce didn't think he could force himself to eat another bite of cheeseburger.

"So, um, Dad, you given any thought to what you're going to do next?"

Relieved at the change of subject, Royce explained his plans to get a teaching certificate and continue to watch Jake while he attended college.

Michael's mouth tightened. "Boy, you've really done a one-eighty about kids, Dad. You never could bear to be around them before. Or was it just me?"

His comment was a knife to Royce's heart. But it was no worse than the pain Michael had felt over the years.

Royce touched his shoulder. "It was never you, Michael. I've always loved you."

"You had a strange way of showing it."

Royce glanced at Jake. He so didn't want to have this conversation in front of Jake, who actually still seemed to hold him in high esteem, despite the fact that he'd bailed earlier.

"I know. I'm sorry." It was inadequate, but what more could he say?

"Yeah, well, it's a case of too little, too late. Besides, it looks like you've got my replacement all picked out." He turned to Jake. "Just don't count on him too much. He'll eventually disappoint you."

Then he stood, threw a wad of bills on the table and grabbed his backpack. "I'll catch a cab back to the airport."

Royce stood. "Michael, don't leave."

Michael's mouth twisted. "Looks like the table's turned. I'm the one leaving this time. Bye, Dad."

And he walked out of the restaurant without a backward glance.

Royce felt as if Michael had ripped out his heart and stomped on it. The worst part was he knew he deserved what he got.

Turning to Jake, he almost cried out at the disillusionment he saw in the boy's eyes. Everyone important to him knew what a failure he was as a father—past and present.

Because that's one thing this meal had pointed out. Both Michael and Jake were the sons of his heart. Too bad he hadn't realized it until it was too late.

KATY STOOD in the hospital parking lot. She was too late. Jake had already been released to Royce's care.

Defeat washed over her. She'd so wanted to be here for her son. But at least Royce had come through.

Why Eddie hadn't taken his son home was anybody's guess. There was a new shift of nurses on duty and they didn't seem to know.

She got into the rental car and headed home, taking the streets a lot slower than she had on Interstate 8 from California. She'd managed to rack up two speeding tickets, but her only concern had been getting home as quickly as possible.

Flipping open her cell phone, she tried Royce again. It still went straight to voice mail. Then she called her home phone, but no answer. She left a message just in case they'd... What? Stepped out for a midnight stroll? Maybe they'd run out to the pharmacy to fill Jake's prescription. That had to be it.

Some of the tension eased from her shoulders. The drive home seemed surreal, as if she'd been gone years instead of days.

Katy looked for Royce's SUV in the complex parking lot, but didn't see it. Surely, they would be home by now. She checked her apartment first, figuring an injured boy would want to sleep in his own bed. But it didn't appear as if anyone had been there for hours.

She jogged out her door and took the stairs two at a time down to the third floor. She pounded on Royce's door, but there wasn't any answer. His neighbor opened her door, though, and glared.

"Have you seen Royce?"

"No." The door slammed shut.

Where could they be?

Katy's heart pounded. Something bad had happened, she just knew it. Her breathing came in short, shallow gasps.

When her breathing slowed, Katy went downstairs to the parking lot. She didn't know what to do. Should she call the police?

*Calm down. It'll be fine.*

There was probably a reasonable explanation. She was just overreacting. No need for panic.

Headlights swept the parking lot as a vehicle pulled in. It was Royce's SUV.

She ran to the passenger side door and wrenched it open.

"Jake!"

## CHAPTER TWENTY-SIX

KATY REMOVED Jake's seat belt and drew the sleepy boy out of the SUV.

"Are you okay, honey?"

"I got a cast. Guess who ate with us?"

Katy's breathing returned to normal at Jake's casual demeanor. It had all been an adventure for him.

"It's a terrific cast." She set him on the ground. "Who ate with you?"

"Michael McIntyre, the famous race-car driver. See, he signed my cast." He raised his right arm.

"Very nice."

She glanced up to find Royce studying her.

"I've been calling your cell."

"Oh, crap, I turned it off when I picked up Jake and forgot to turn it back on. I meant to call you, but things got so crazy."

"I'm his mother. I would have thought that trumped the other crazy things. I—I was worried sick when I couldn't find you two." Tears gathered in her eyes. She was suddenly very, very tired.

Royce came around the car and pulled her into his arms. "It's okay."

"I wasn't there when he needed me. I should have been there. Then you left him alone in the hospital."

"I left him with his father."

It felt right to be cocooned in Royce's reassuring warmth. But there was something different about him. A reserve that hadn't been there before.

She leaned back to look at his face. Lines of tension bracketed his mouth. "What's wrong?" she asked.

"It's been a long day. Long night."

"Michael was with you?"

Royce nodded. "He flew in for a couple hours to see me."

"How did it go?"

Jake said, "Michael told Royce he was a crummy dad and left to get a cab. He told me Royce would disappoint me, too. But he's wrong. Royce is the best. Even though he kinda broke his promise at the hospital."

Backing a step, she said, "Your day sounded very, um, eventful."

"You could call it that." His eyes narrowed. "What?"

"Nothing."

"Tell me. Something's on your mind."

"Now's not the time to discuss it."

"Why not?" He angled his head toward Jake. "He's pretty much heard everything else today."

"I did some soul-searching on the drive from California. Maybe we rushed into this thing with you and me. It's awfully soon after your accident and you're trying to get your life back on track. I wouldn't blame you if you weren't sure what you wanted."

"I want you, Katy. But Michael feels I'm trying to replace him with Jake…and maybe he's right. Eddie made a similar remark. What if I'm trying to rewrite history through you and Jake?"

"What're you saying?"

"I care about you and Jake more than I ever could have imagined. But you're right, we jumped into this thing without thinking. My first priority has to be rebuilding my relationship with Michael. He's right, I always put him after everything else. This time, I need to put him first. At least until we've reestablished a relationship."

Why hadn't she seen it? Jake reminded Royce of Michael so, of course, he was drawn to him. And by extension, drawn to her? The thought made her slightly nauseous.

She was too exhausted to find a reserve of tact. "I guess you've found the perfect excuse to bail on us. Something scared you and you won't admit it."

"Today just showed that I'm not the guy you want there in an emergency. I'll always do the wrong thing. I'm just grateful I didn't hurt Jake more by moving him."

"You did what most people would do. But I need to know you're there one hundred percent for Jake when I'm gone. Tonight destroyed that faith." She took a deep, fortifying breath. "I hope you understand that it's not a good idea for you to continue as his nanny."

Pain flashed quickly in Royce's eyes, then

it was gone. "Of course. How quickly do you think you can find a replacement?"

Katy longed to make it a fast, clean cut. But reality had shown her finding a replacement nanny could take time.

"I'll make every effort to find someone within two weeks. Will that be acceptable for you?"

"Yes."

"Come on, Jake, let's go."

Jake didn't move. "I don't want anyone else. I want Royce. This is stupid. You guys are being stupid."

"It's just not working out, Jake." She wrapped her arm around his shoulder and started guiding him toward the apartment.

Royce walked alongside them. "Here's his pain medication and the release instructions from the hospital."

She accepted the items.

Royce touched her arm. "And Katy?"

"Yes?"

"I'm sorry. About everything."

"Me, too." Her voice was husky with unshed tears. It seemed she'd cried more in the past twenty-four hours than the past several years combined.

A COUPLE OF DAYS LATER, Royce answered his cell. "Hey, Becca. What's up?"

"I was going to ask you the same thing. Do I need to come out there?"

"Everything's fine," he lied. "Why?"

"I called Michael and he says you two had some kind of fight. You've never argued before."

"He was never a grown man with a pile of resentments before." There, it felt good to tell it the way he saw it, without beating himself up every second. Then he told her about Michael's visit and his son's reaction to Jake.

"This stuff would have come out sooner or later, Royce. Your relationship with Jake just brought it out sooner."

"There is no relationship with Jake. I'm his nanny, nothing more. And in less than two weeks I won't even be that."

"No relationship? All I've heard is Jake this and Jake that. Along with a lot of references to Katy. Where's she fit into all this?"

"We kind of got together, then decided to cool it."

"Why?"

"Michael did have a point that I might be trying to rewrite history through Jake and Katy."

"Bull. Michael is a fabulous man. But he's also a man who didn't see his father a lot while he was growing up—"

"I said—"

"I know you're sorry, Royce. I was in Germany and saw the tears running down your face after you realized you didn't recognize your own son. You managed to cover, but I knew what was going on."

"How could I not recognize him?"

"In your mind, he's still a kid, because you didn't see him day in, day out."

Clearing his throat, Royce said, "I know I was a crummy father. I've said I was sorry and I'll keep on saying it."

"Why?"

"What?"

"Why keep saying it?"

"Because he hasn't forgiven me yet."

"So all this self-flagellation will bring that

about more quickly? Or do you simply enjoy punishing yourself? Seems pretty convenient that you finally commit to a woman for the first time in twenty-five years—"

"Hey, I've had women—"

Becca sighed. "Yes, I'm well aware you've 'had' women in that time. But you haven't committed your heart. Unless something happened overseas I don't know about."

"No. I usually tell you the important stuff."

"Sounds to me like you're using Michael as an excuse to back away from Katy and her son. Relationships are scary and messy and with baggage thrown in, probably downright impossible at times."

"This goes beyond that. I owe Michael."

"Are you going to live the rest of your life according to Michael's wants and desires because you screwed up five, ten, twenty years ago?"

"If it will make things up to him."

"Oh, Royce, you poor bastard. Michael won't accept your apology and move on until he's damn good and ready. And it really has very little to do with whom you decide to build your life with. You can become a monk and keep telling him you're sorry until you're blue in the face and it won't make a difference."

He didn't bother to temper the sarcasm in his voice when he said, "Then what, oh wise sister, does it take?"

"He needs to *want* to forgive. And you need to live your life based on integrity and love."

"You're saying nothing I can do is enough?"

"Not unless he wants to forgive you. So you might as well live a full, happy life while showing him how much he means to you. Because there are no guarantees where kids are concerned."

Royce felt as if she'd smacked him upside the head with a two-by-four. "When did you get so smart, little sister?"

"Always have been, big brother."

"Thanks, I owe you one for the tough love."

"Good. You can watch my kids while Gabriel and I take a cruise next year for our anniversary."

He chuckled. "No way. That's what you've got in-laws living with you for."

"Yeah, but I'll need someone to supervise them, too. Now, go make your life as big, and fun and loving as the mess I have here."

"Love you, Becca."

"Love you, too."

KATY SHUT DOWN her computer at work and closed her eyes, rubbing her temples. She'd just done cursory online background checks on potential nannies and the results scared her. One woman had several drug convictions and another was apparently living out of her car.

Grabbing her purse, she headed home.

The aroma of garlic tantalized her from the moment she exited the elevator. She sniffed appreciatively, her stomach growling in response.

Royce hadn't cooked since they'd agreed Jake needed a different nanny. He'd been cool and professional, keeping her abreast of Jake's homework and activities, but not sharing anything personal.

She missed him. Missed his laughter and warmth, the way he hugged her so freely, his constant, quiet support. Missed making love with him.

Unlocking the door, her heart skipped a beat at the sight that greeted her. The table was set for two, complete with a tablecloth and candles. Wine rested in the holder.

"Hey, you're home." Royce sounded as if he was actually glad to see her.

"What's all this?"

Jake rushed out of his room, a duffel bag slung over his shoulder. "Hi, Mom. Grandma's coming for me in a minute. I'm gonna spend the night at her house. She doesn't want you sad anymore and she thinks Royce can make you happy."

"You are? Royce, what's this all about? I can't believe my mom would spring something like this on me."

"But you see, she likes me, especially once I convinced her I'm done making you sad. Your mother's a tough cookie, and believe me it took a lot of convincing. And a plate of Rice Krispies Treats." Royce's eyes sparkled with mischief.

"Grandma's gonna take me to school tomorrow, too. She said you might be busy.

And after school, we're gonna take a plane and go to Disneyland for the weekend."

Katy frowned. "Why do I get the feeling I'm being set up?"

"Because you are. You have no choice but to give in gracefully and enjoy."

"I don't like being manipulated."

Royce opened the wine and poured two glasses. He handed one to her.

"Thank you," she murmured reflexively. "I mean it, Royce, you can't just waltz in here and take over my life as if nothing happened."

"What do you think of the wine?"

Katy sipped it, enjoying the flavor, remembering the last time she'd shared a bottle of this particular wine with Royce. It had been the night of Jake's birthday party.

"It's lovely. But it's not working."

He laughed. "Then drink up."

Damn. The man was irresistible when he set his mind to it.

There was a knock at the door.

"That's Grandma." Jake opened the door as Katy started to protest.

Her mother said hello and whisked Jake away before Katy had a chance to respond.

She turned, planting her hands on her hips. "What's this all about?"

"Let's sit down." He gestured toward the couch with his wineglass.

Katy selected a seat, sipping her wine warily. "I thought we had an understanding."

"No, we had a *mis*understanding. What I'm trying to do is work our way back to understanding."

"Have you been drinking all afternoon?"

"Nope, this is my first glass."

Katy leaned back, enjoying his company in spite of feeling like a yo-yo.

"How was your day?" he asked.

Rolling her eyes, she said, "Don't you have anything better than that?"

"I thought we'd get the formalities out of the way first." He smiled, but she detected a bit of nervousness in his voice.

She tried hard not to be charmed. "My job is…comfortable, familiar. I'm grateful to be there, it's almost like a second home. But I wanted…more."

"And you could have had it, if we hadn't jerked the rug out from under you."

Katy shrugged, unwilling to allow him to

see how much the job with Sinclair had meant to her. "There'll be other jobs."

"Absolutely. But I wanted you to know how sorry I was for not supporting you one hundred percent."

"You were mostly supportive."

"I mean with Jake. I should have encouraged you to finish the auction, reassured you that I had everything under control on the home front. Truth is, I'm not always the best parent in charge during a crisis situation. I tend to freak out."

Hurt warred with irritation. "Funny you didn't mention that when you agreed to be my nanny."

"It was only temporary, remember? Besides, as nanny I could just call you or the paramedics and my job was done. Saturday night Jake needed a parent. And I happened to be the closest thing available given Eddie's circumstances."

"Did I expect too much of you?" Her voice was low. She'd worried about that, wondering if she'd jumped to conclusions after they'd slept together. But he'd told her he adored her.

"No, absolutely not."

He set his glass down on the coffee table. "My sister called today. Becca pretty much called me an ass, among other things."

"I think I'd like her."

"I'm sure you will like her. You two are very similar in some ways. Anyway, she'd talked to Michael and wanted to find out about our fight."

"What'd she think?"

"That I need to quit beating myself up. That Michael may or may not forgive me and the best thing I can do is live my life with integrity while still letting him know how much I love him."

"But you thought Jake and I might come between you and Michael…. I'd never want to do that."

Royce touched her cheek. "You won't. Katy, you are everything good and beautiful in my life. You're smart, honest and loving and I've missed you like crazy."

They'd seen each other almost every day, but she understood exactly what he meant. He missed their closeness, their connection.

Katy rested her face against his palm, absorbing the warmth of his touch. "I've missed you, too," she murmured.

"Can we pick up where we left off?"

"I'm tempted, so tempted. I love what we had together, Royce. But I can't rely on you like I thought I could. I'll always be wondering if you're going to let me down again at some important time."

"You know, that'll always be my biggest fear, too. I love you. I love Jake. And I'm ready for a commitment. And maybe we can balance our strengths and weaknesses to make a family that works."

"How?"

"Just know that I'm not so good in the kid illness and injury areas, but better in others. We complement each other, if we allow it. I do birthday parties and Rice Krispies Treats, you do boo-boo kissing and barf patrol."

Katy couldn't help but laugh. "Strange as it may seem, I think I'd be getting the good end of the deal."

"See, we're perfect for each other." He held her gaze, his voice husky when he said, "And I can promise you one thing, I will love you with my whole heart to the end of my days. And I'll be the very best stepfather for Jake that I can be. Marry me?"

Katy brushed tears off her face. "If it were just me, I'd be willing to take the chance. But what if you disappoint Jake?"

"I guess the odds are that, as a stepfather, I'm bound to disappoint him at some time. But he's old enough to tell me when I've done something wrong and we'll work it out like any other family. Please say you'll take a chance on me? On us?"

Cupping his face with her hand, she kissed him. "I love you, Royce."

He beamed. "And you'll marry me? We'll become a real family?"

Katy smiled. "I think maybe we've been a real family for a while, we just didn't know it. Yes, I would love to marry you and spend the rest of my life with you."

Just then, they heard a tapping on the apartment door, which appeared to be cracked open slightly.

Katy stood, but Royce pulled her back down.

"Listen."

"Morse code?"

He nodded. "Y-A-Y! I think we have Jake's vote of approval."

Laughing, she said, "Yes, it seems so. Now which one of us gets to tackle the eavesdropping issue with him?"

"As long as there's no blood or vomit involved, I'll catch this one."

"Deal."

Royce kissed her, slowly, persuasively. "But after he gets back from Disneyland."

"Good decision," she murmured against his mouth, throwing her arms around his neck and pulling him close.

## EPILOGUE

*Three years later...*

KATY GRASPED THE ENDS of Royce's tie and
pulled him close, enjoying the opportunity to
kiss him. "Mmm. I like kissing an artist."

"Save that thought for later. Right now
I'm too nervous to give you the appropriate
attention that statement requires."

Glancing around, she said, "The Industrial Arts room looks great. Just like a real
art gallery."

"You think so?"

"Absolutely. Your crew did a good job."

"Under the direction of my wife, of
course."

"Don't forget, I helped." Jake sauntered
over, standing shoulder to shoulder with her.
She couldn't quite get over how his voice

had deepened recently. At fourteen, he didn't seem to be her baby anymore.

He glanced at Royce's left arm. "Decided to go au naturel?"

Royce nodded. "Yep, the prosthesis just isn't me, no pun intended."

"Your tie's crooked, Jake. I'll help you after I get Royce's tie done."

"I can get it. Go back to your mushy stuff."

"Well, since I have your permission." She stood on tiptoe and kissed Royce one more time. "There. Now let me get that tie."

He loosely draped his arms around her waist as she worked. Leaning close, he said, "Have I told you recently I love you?"

"Not in the last hour."

"I do."

She smiled up at him. "Your students will be arriving any minute. Go do your thing and we'll meet up after the showing."

"No way, lady, you're not getting away. I want you by my side."

"Always." But when his students arrived, she slipped to the background to watch.

Her time to be front and center was as the new auctioneer at Parker Family Auctions.

With Royce's blessing, she'd gone to a two-week intensive auction calling school. And when Herb had needed his second knee surgery, she'd stepped in to fill the void. Now, she and Herb job shared and she couldn't have been happier.

Katy smiled as the students joked with Royce. They greeted him as a friend, but there was respect, too. Royce loved teaching and the kids obviously thought he was great.

"Hey, dude, that chemistry test on Friday was brutal," one boy remarked.

"I don't want you blowing up my lab, kid. Look what happened last time a student forgot certain chlorides don't mix well with burning methyl alcohol." Royce raised his left arm and laughed. The kids laughed, too.

"Hey, you got that in Russia, so don't try to scam us."

Another boy asked, "Mr. McIntyre, what if people say our work sucks?"

"They won't. You guys—" he nodded to the two female students "—and ladies are a talented bunch. I'm so impressed with everything you've done this semester. I'm grateful Mr. Jones allowed me to sponsor the new Industrial Arts Club. You kids have given me the opportunity to combine two things I love—working with you and creating beauty with metal."

"Hey, we did all the work."

"You sure did. But I've been dabbling a bit on the side, myself." Royce removed the cover from a metal sculpture that was beautiful in its stark simplicity. "I call it *Love*."

He held Katy's gaze and smiled.

She nodded, unable to take her eyes off her handsome husband.

"So that's what he's been working on in the garage," Jake murmured.

Katy blinked back tears. For a guy who once thought his life was over, Royce had sure found a way back. And given her the kind of life she'd never thought possible. She meant to tell him the minute the crowd dispersed.

But it didn't start to thin for hours. Parents, students, local press and government officials—each was overwhelmingly supportive of the industrial artists and their craft.

One man studied Royce's sculpture for quite a while. When he turned, she held her breath.

*Michael.*

Katy watched as he approached his father. She followed behind, ready to support Royce if things didn't go well.

"Great show, Dad." Michael extended his hand.

Royce smiled, grasping his son's hand. After a brief handshake and a moment's hesitation he pulled him into a hug.

Michael's posture seemed to relax. Katy just hoped both men could find a way to a positive relationship. Royce had made great strides in forgiving himself. Every teen he helped in class seemed to erase a little more of his shame. And he couldn't have been a better stepfather to Jake.

Now it was Michael's turn to forgive.

"I'm so glad you're here," Royce said. "I wasn't sure if you received my invitation."

"Yeah, I did. Obviously. Sorry I didn't make it to your wedding. I had a race."

"Sure, I understand. Are you going to be in town for a while?"

"We just stopped off today on our way back to Charlotte."

"We? Your crew?"

Michael chuckled and Katy was captivated. He had Royce's smile.

"I guess you could call them my crew." He motioned to someone standing in the doorway. "This is my fiancée, Tina, and her son, Alex. Soon to be my son, too."

A petite blonde and a little redheaded boy stepped forward and shook Royce's hand. The boy appeared to be about four and was obviously wearing his Sunday best. He pulled at the collar of his dress shirt.

"Katy, come here. I want you to meet Tina and Alex. This is my wife, Katy."

When all the introductions were complete, an uncomfortable silence fell.

Michael cleared his throat. "Um, Dad, Alex was asking me the other day if I knew how to make Rice Krispies Treats and I had to admit I didn't have a clue. But I told him his Grandpa Royce has the reputation for being a champion maker. So we thought maybe you might give us your recipe."

"I'll do better than that." Royce glanced at his watch. "It's still fairly early. Why don't you come back to our house and I'll walk you through it? We might even get

Jake to help. And, of course, we'll have to sample the results."

"Who's Jake?" the boy asked.

"He's my stepson and that's how I met Jake's mom. It's a funny story I can tell you while we make the treats."

Alex tucked his hand in Royce's and smiled. "I like Grandpa Royce."

"So is it a plan?" Royce glanced from Michael to Tina.

Michael said, "Yeah, it's a plan."

Katy blinked back tears. This was truly an evening they would remember forever.

* * * * *

*Look for Becca's story,*
*BABY, I'M YOURS,*
*in March 2008.*

Melita had been expecting a chaste quick kiss of the generic variety. But this kiss with Sully was the kind that sparked a dying flame to life. The kind of kiss you can't plan for. The kind of kiss memories are built on.

The memory of her murdered lover, Nemo, came to her then and she made a starved little noise in the back of her throat. She raised her arms and threaded her fingers through Sully's hair, pulled him closer. Felt his body settle, then melt into her.

In that instant her hunger for him grew, and his for her. She pressed herself to him with more urgency, and he responded in kind.

Melita came out of her kiss-induced memory of Nemo with a start. "Wait a minute." She pushed Sully away from her. "You bastard!"

She spit two nasty words at him in Greek, then wiped his kiss from her lips.

"I thought you deserved some solid proof that I'm still in one piece." He started for the door. "The clock's ticking, honey. Come on, let's get out of here."

"That's it? You sucker me into kissing you, and that's all you have to say?"

"I'm sorry. How's that?"

He didn't sound sorry in the least. "You're—"

"Getting out of this godforsaken prison cell. Stop whining and let's go."

"Not if I was being shot at sunrise. Go. You deserve whatever you get if you walk out that door."

He turned back. "Freedom is what I'm going to get."

"A second of freedom before the guards in the hall shoot you." She jammed her hands on her hips. "And to think I was worried about you."

"If you're staying behind, it's no skin off my ass."

"Wait! What about our deal?"

"You just said you're not coming. Make up your mind."

"Have you forgotten we need a boat?"

"How could I? You keep harping on it."

"I'm not going without a boat. And those guards out there aren't going to just let you walk out of here. You need me and we need a plan."

"I already have a plan. I'm getting out of here. That's the plan."

"I should have realized that you never intended to take me with you from the very beginning. You're a liar and a coward."

Of everything she had read, there was nothing in Sully Paxton's file that hinted he was a coward, but it was the one word that seemed to register in that one-track mind of his. The look he nailed her with a second later was pure venom.

He came at her so quickly she didn't have time to get out of his way. "You know I'm not a coward."

"Prove it. Give me until dawn. I need one more night to put everything in place before we leave the island."

"You're asking me to stay in this cell one more night...and trust you?"

"Yes."

He snorted. "Yesterday you knew they were planning to harm me, but instead of doing something about it you went to bed and never gave me a second thought. Suppose tonight you do the same. By tomorrow I might damn well be in my grave."

"Okay, I screwed up. I won't do it again." Melita sucked in a ragged breath. "I can't leave this minute. Dawn, Sully. Wait until dawn." When he looked as if he was about to say no, she pleaded, "Please wait for me."

"You're asking a lot. The door's open now. I would be a fool to hang around here and trust that you'll be back."

"What you can trust is that I want off this island as badly as you do, and you're my only hope."

"I must be crazy."

"Is that a yes?"

"Dammit!" He turned his back on her. Swore twice more.

"You won't be sorry."

He turned around. "I already am. How about we seal this new deal?"

He was staring at her lips. Suddenly Melita knew what he expected. "We already sealed it."

"One more. You enjoyed it. Admit it."

"I enjoyed it because I was kissing someone else."

He laughed. "That's a good one."

"It's true. It might have been your lips, but it wasn't you I was kissing."

"If that's your excuse for wanting to kiss me, then—"

"I was kissing Nemo."

"What's a nemo?"

Melita gave Sully a look that clearly told him that he was trespassing on sacred ground. She was about to enforce it with a warning when a voice in the hall jerked them both to attention.

She bolted away from the wall. "Get back in bed. Hurry. I'll be here before dawn."

She didn't reach the door before he snagged her arm, pulled her up against him and planted a kiss on her lips that took her completely by surprise.

When he released her, he said, "If you're confused about who just kissed you, the name's Sully. I'll be here waiting at dawn. Don't be late."

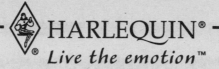

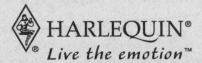

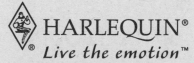

# HARLEQUIN®
# INTRIGUE®

## BREATHTAKING ROMANTIC SUSPENSE

Shared dangers and passions lead to electrifying
romance and heart-stopping suspense!

Every month, you'll meet six new heroes
who are guaranteed to make your spine tingle
and your pulse pound. With them you'll enter
into the exciting world of Harlequin Intrigue—
where your life is on the line
and so is your heart!

## THAT'S INTRIGUE—
## ROMANTIC SUSPENSE
## AT ITS BEST!

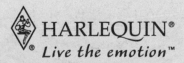

## HARLEQUIN®
### *Live the emotion*™

![Harlequin Historical logo] **Harlequin® Historical**
Historical Romantic Adventure!

*Imagine a time of chivalrous
knights and unconventional ladies,
roguish rakes and impetuous
heiresses, rugged cowboys
and spirited frontierswomen—
these rich and vivid tales will
capture your imagination!*

*Harlequin Historical . . .
they're too good to miss!*

HHDIR06

# HARLEQUIN®
## *Presents*

**The world's bestselling romance series...**
**The series that brings you your favorite authors,**
**month after month:**

Helen Bianchin...Emma Darcy
Lynne Graham...Penny Jordan
Miranda Lee...Sandra Marton
Anne Mather...Carole Mortimer
Susan Napier...Michelle Reid

**and many more uniquely talented authors!**

Wealthy, powerful, gorgeous men...
Women who have feelings just like your own...
The stories you love, set in exotic, glamorous locations...

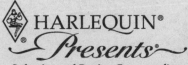

# HARLEQUIN®
## *Presents*

**Seduction and Passion Guaranteed!**

HPDIR1

*passionate powerful provocative love stories*

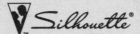

## Silhouette Desire delivers strong heroes, spirited heroines and compelling love stories.

Desire features your favorite authors, including

# Annette Broadrick, Diana Palmer, Maureen Child and Brenda Jackson.

### Passionate, powerful and provocative romances *guaranteed!*

For superlative authors, sensual stories and sexy heroes, choose Silhouette Desire.

*passionate powerful provocative love stories*